"You're the nasty Santa?"

Her words came out harsher and louder than she'd intended.

To his credit, Reid Evanson looked as shocked as she was at the unexpected turn.

"What are you doing here?" she demanded.

"You're the one who asked for me."

"I didn't. I asked to see Santa Claus."

Without another word, he stepped around the long, highly polished counter and gently took her by the elbow. "Let's discuss all this in my office."

His office? "You run the resort," she commented as he shut the door behind him.

"I own it. Along with my partner, Alex."

The pieces started to fall into place. She remembered now that Reid came from a wealthy family of hoteliers.

Suddenly, it was all too much. Far from fleeing her unpleasant associations with the holiday as it related to her failed relationship, she'd somehow ended up face-to-face with someone who'd played a major role in the whole fiasco.

Reid had been her ex-fiancé's best man. And she knew he'd never thought her good enough for his buddy.

Dear Reader,

The holiday season is always a joyous time for me. But no one can argue that December can often be stressful and chaotic. That's certainly the case for Celeste Frajedi.

Celeste feels the need to get away every December to avoid the holidays altogether. What should be a joyous time of year only reminds her of the disastrous Christmas wedding she was supposed to have, where she was instead left at the altar.

This year she finds herself on the beautiful island of Jamaica. She also finds herself face-to-face with a man she'd hoped never to see again.

Reid Evanson was the best man at her nonwedding all those years ago. And they've never forgiven each other for the past. The only thing to do is avoid each other at all costs.

Somehow, shockingly, they find themselves falling in love instead. Sometimes, all it takes is a little holiday magic to make the season joyful again.

Nina

Their Festive Island Escape

—

Nina Singh

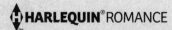 HARLEQUIN® ROMANCE

Recycling programs
for this product may
not exist in your area.

ISBN-13: 978-1-335-49961-5

Their Festive Island Escape

First North American publication 2019

Copyright © 2019 by Nilay Nina Singh

Printed in U.S.A.

Nina Singh lives just outside Boston, Massachusetts, with her husband, children and a very rambunctious Yorkie. After several years in the corporate world, she finally followed the advice of family and friends to "give the writing a go, already." She's oh-so-happy she did. When not at her keyboard, she likes to spend time on the tennis court or golf course. Or immersed in a good read.

Books by Nina Singh

Harlequin Romance

Destination Brides

Swept Away by the Venetian Millionaire

The Men Who Make Christmas

Snowed in with the Reluctant Tycoon

9 to 5

Miss Prim and the Maverick Millionaire

The Marriage of Inconvenience
Reunited with Her Italian Billionaire
Tempted by Her Island Millionaire
Christmas with Her Secret Prince
Captivated by the Millionaire

Visit the Author Profile page at Harlequin.com.

To my children, you make every vacation and holiday nothing less than a gift

CHAPTER ONE

HER SISTER JUST didn't get it. But then again, Celeste had never really been able to get through to her when it came to the holidays. Or through to her mother, for that matter. Her family would never understand. Not that she really understood them in return.

"I can't believe you haven't moved on yet," Tara declared, throwing her hands up in the air. "Your wedding was three years ago. Get over it already."

Tara wasn't often accused of being overly sensitive. For the wedding her sister had so callously just referred to had never actually happened. Celeste bit down on a frustrated groan. She really was in no mood to talk about this. She didn't even want to think about the day she'd been so humiliatingly left at the altar, waiting for a groom who had never bothered to show up.

The humiliation still haunted her nightmares—

dozens of pitying eyes staring at her as the minutes ticked by.

She was supposed to have been a Christmas bride. Instead she'd been a jilted one.

How did Tara not understand that she wanted nothing to do with the holiday now? How did she not see that the best thing to do for her mental health was just to get away from the city until the whole season was over?

Her sister's next question only proved that she didn't understand Celeste at all.

"How can you leave your family and just take off to the islands every year? Christmas just isn't the same without you here."

Celeste couldn't help the pang of guilt that landed in her gut. Perhaps one day she'd be able to put all of it behind her. Maybe she'd even enjoy the holidays again at some future point in time. She just wasn't there yet. Nowhere near, in fact. Every street decoration, every holiday jingle, every sidewalk corner Santa only reminded her of Jack and the days leading up to her abject humiliation.

Not to mention, her sister's seeming disappointment held a secondary layer. On the surface, Tara sounded like a caring, loving sibling who just wanted to spend the holidays with her older sister. But there was more to it than that. At the age of twenty-six, Tara was much too dependent on her older sister financially. And so was their mother, for that matter.

Celeste knew she should have curbed that dependence long before. Especially given all that it had cost her three years ago. But her sense of duty and responsibility as the only financially stable member of her family often overrode her good sense. Something had broken in her mother when their father had abandoned them over a decade ago, leaving nothing behind but his debts. Wendy had never fully recovered. And Tara had taken it just as hard. It had been left to Celeste as the older sibling to try to pick up the pieces.

She was still doing so. By now it was second nature. Which wasn't exactly a sound reason to keep doing it, but she couldn't exactly turn her back on either of them. Especially considering Tara was a mother herself now. Besides, wasn't one of the reasons Celeste had worked so hard to be able to help out her always cash-strapped family members?

"I thought for sure you'd stay around this year, sis." Tara's voice was petulant and whiny.

"Why would you think that?"

"Because your usual resort is nothing but a pile of damaged debris."

She spoke the truth. The last hurricane season had nearly destroyed the island that housed

Celeste's yearly destination spot. After her devastating non-wedding, Celeste had chosen to continue on and attend her already-paid-for Caribbean honeymoon on a luxe tropical resort. She'd been going back to the same location every December since. This year, that island was sadly not an option.

Celeste had been heartbroken thinking of the usual staff and how they'd lost their livelihoods. She'd been regularly donating to various charities in charge of rebuilding, wished she could do more. In the meantime, she'd had to choose an unfamiliar resort on a different island. Apparently, her family had been counting on her canceling the trip altogether.

Never mind that she'd called weeks ago to tell both her sister and her mother of her exact plans.

Honestly, it was as if they didn't know her at all.

It would take more than a natural disaster to keep her in Manhattan over the holidays. She wanted nothing to do with Christmas, would skip the entire month of December if she possibly could. The non-stop carols, the sparkling decorations all over the city, the hustling and bustling crowds within a mile of any shopping center. It all overwhelmed and irritated her to no end. Even the usually quiet and cozy café they sat in was now a crowded mess of harried shoppers carrying all manner of bags and parcels.

And none of that even had anything to do with the bad memories of her broken engagement. That only added a whole other layer of distaste.

Bah humbug and all that.

Across the square wooden table, Tara's lower lip actually did a little quiver. For the briefest moment, Celeste couldn't help but feel touched. Tara had her faults, but Celeste knew deep down that her little sister really did miss her over the holidays. Tara just wasn't one to show much emotion. No wonder, given the way they'd had to grow up. Though that quality had seemed to be slowly softening since she'd become a mother.

"I was hoping we could go in on Mom's gift together," Tara continued. "You know, split the cost." She glanced downward toward the floor. "Money's a little tight for me right now, and you just got that promotion…"

The usual hint of guilt tugged within her chest.

Celeste wasn't going to bother to point out that "going in together" most often meant she would be footing the whole cost of their mother's gift and the holiday dinner. But what was there to do? The truth was, Celeste really was much better off than her sister. As was usually the case. Still, it was a fact that couldn't exactly be ignored.

Besides, Celeste didn't have it in her to discuss it much further. She had to get home and start packing. She reached for her purse and pulled out her checkbook, started scribbling after deciding on an amount, then handed it to her only sibling.

"Here, this should cover the cost of Mom's gift and a nice dinner out for the two of you. As well as a little extra so that you can pick up something for yourself," she added, despite the fact that she'd already handed Tara the holiday gift she'd purchased for her as soon as they'd sat down—a pair of fourteen-karat gold teardrop earrings she'd meticulously wrapped herself in bright, colorful paper and ribbons. Looked like Tara's guilt trip about her leaving to go on holiday was indeed working.

Tara's lips quivered ever so slightly and her eyes grew shiny as she reached for the check. "Thanks, sis. I'm going to find a way to pay you back one of these days. Once I figure out how to get on my own two feet."

Celeste gave her hand a squeeze. "I know you will," she reassured, despite her own doubt.

Tara smiled. "Hope you have a good trip. See you when you get back."

* * *

Even under the bulky, stuffed red flannel suit, it was clear the man who wore it was no regular Santa. No, this man was definitely not old, rotund or particularly jolly. Though Celeste could tell he was trying hard to fit the part. Couldn't the resort have found a better-fitting actor to play the role? Even from this distance where she sat on her lounge chair, she could tell Santa was tall and fit. His piercing dark eyes held no jolly old twinkle, though they did seem to catch the sunlight as he shifted his gaze from one child to the next as he handed out presents from his burly, oversize sack. An odd sensation of déjà vu nagged at her. Something about the pretend Santa seemed oddly familiar. Probably just her imagination.

The kids didn't seem to notice how ill-suited he was for the role, they were all laughing loudly and scurrying to open the gifts they'd just been handed.

Celeste flipped the page of the paperback she'd picked up at the airport and returned her attention to the story. Or she tried to, anyway. The kids were pretty noisy. The scene before her was charming and sweet—Santa sent to the beach to entertain and bestow gifts upon the youngest guests. It reminded her of everything she'd once so foolishly longed for. Exactly the kind of scene she was trying to get away from when she jetted out to the Caribbean every December. She was here for warm and tropical. Not stark reminders of all she'd lost three years ago when the man she'd loved, the man she'd dreamed of having children with like the ones currently in front of her, had so callously deserted her at the worst possible moment.

This resort was definitely geared more toward families than the one she was used to. She might have to find a more remote section of beach in order to avoid such scenes for the rest of her stay. Her heart couldn't take it.

A shadow suddenly fell over the pages of her book.

"Ho-ho-ho."

Santa appeared to be strolling the beach closer and closer to where she sat, the children following close behind him. Now they all stood just a couple of feet from her chair. She watched as St. Nicholas leaned down to tousle the hair of one particularly excited young boy who'd clearly just received some type of toy car based on the wrapped shape.

It was futile. There was no way to even try to concentrate on her romantic suspense novel now. As charming as the children were, and they really were adorable, she couldn't take much more Christmas cheer. Glancing down the expanse of sand, she searched in vain for another empty beach chair farther away from this main part of the resort. They all appeared taken. With a resigned sigh, Celeste dropped the book and stood, wrapping her silky sarong around her midsection. Might as well get another cup of coffee or perhaps a latte until all the commotion quieted.

A squealing toddler darted past her to get to the faux Santa and she nearly toppled over in her effort to avoid the collision. This was so far from the relaxing morning she'd envisioned. Not that the kids weren't cute. They really were, with all their excitement and near tangible anticipation to receive a present. They were just so… loud. Loud, boisterous reminders of all she'd be missing out on in life. Look at how her one attempt to start a family had turned out; nothing more than an abject lesson in humiliation and hurt.

No, she wouldn't be having children. Or her own family. The one she'd been born into took up more than enough of her time and emotional energy.

She leaned down to retrieve her flip-flops from beneath the lounge chair and stopped short when she straightened. A wall of bright red topped by a cotton white beard suddenly filled her view.

"Ho-ho-ho. Well, hello there, young lady." Santa smiled at her.

"Um…hi."

"We appear to have disturbed your morning, miss. A big jolly apology for the nuisance."

His words were cordial enough. But Celeste had the clear impression that he was somehow mocking her.

"No apology necessary, St. Nick," she said with a slight salute, then tried to step around him, only to have him block her path. Of all the nerve.

The smile grew wider under the thick fake beard. "Really? I mean, you practically have a circular thought bubble above your head that screams 'bah humbug.'"

The same strange sensation of familiarity nagged at her yet again. He was clearly deepening his voice for the role but something about the tone and inflection rang a bell. And the eyes. As she studied their golden depths she couldn't help but sense that she'd somehow gazed upon those eyes before.

Had she met him before in a professional capacity? Her position as VP of marketing for a luxury goods firm had her regularly working on advertising campaigns with various agencies. Maybe Santa had done work previously as a character actor for a project she'd worked on in the past.

What were the chances?

Not that it mattered. Right now all that mattered was that she find some peace and quiet.

But St. Nick seemed to have other plans.

"Excuse me."

Reid knew he should have stepped away the first time she'd said it. But he couldn't seem to help himself. He'd recognized her immediately. She clearly didn't remember Reid in return. He wondered if her cutting look of utter disdain would change at all if she did recall who he was. No doubt it would intensify. They hadn't exactly been on the best of terms the last time they'd seen each other.

Well, the feeling was mutual.

The children scattered all at once, clearly bored with the conversation the adults were having above their heads.

"I didn't realize they'd hired someone to play the part of Scrooge this morning," he goaded her, not even sure why he was doing so. There really was no reason to try to get a rise out of her. Other than for his pure entertainment.

She sucked in a breath. "I'm sorry. I somehow missed the part where my holiday spirit was any of your business."

He shrugged. "We just aim to please every guest, is all."

She folded her arms across her chest. "And this is how you go about doing so? Aren't you overstepping your responsibility just a bit? You're here simply to hand out some presents to the children." She pointed to the empty fleece sack he held. "Clearly your task is over."

Wow, she really was something else. She may as well have flicked him away like a royal princess dismissing a lowly jester. Not that he didn't look the part in this ridiculous suit.

"Furthermore, I fail to see how my satisfaction is the responsibility of the resort Santa." She studied him up and down. Clearly, he came up lacking in her summation. He should have walked away long before. Or never approached her in the first place. Life was too short to deal with the likes of Miss Frajedi. He had too much on his plate trying to get this place in order.

Still, Reid found himself studying her closely. The past three years had been extremely kind to her, she was still strikingly attractive. Dark, wavy hair framed a strong face with high cheekbones and hazel eyes the color of a Caribbean sunset. No wonder Jack had fallen for her so hard, the poor man. Luckily, he'd come to his senses in time. Though Reid had never approved of the way his friend had ultimately ended things. So last-minute. So hurtful. It was never right to leave a lady at the altar. Not even one like Celeste Frajedi. He'd made sure to share that sentiment with his friend, resulting in a now strained relationship between the men.

Her eyes suddenly narrowed on his face. "Do I know you?" she demanded.

Reid hesitated. For the briefest moment, he debated telling her exactly who he was. The look on her face when she found out would be a sight to see.

Ultimately, he decided against it. What would be the point? She was a paying guest after all. She was entitled to the tropical vacation she had paid for. The resort was large and expansive. The beach alone covered over a mile. If he played his cards right, they would never have to run into each other again for the duration of her stay. In fact, he vowed to make sure of it.

He shrugged. "Everyone knows me. I'm Santa Claus."

She studied him some more. Part of him wanted her to figure it out. Finally, she blew out a deep breath. "Right. Well, Santa. I'd like to go get a cup of coffee." With that, she brushed against his arm in her haste to get past him. An enticing scent of coconut and sun-kissed skin tickled his nose. Some kind of static electricity shot through his elbow and clear down his side.

"Merry Christmas, princess."

He spoke to her back as she stormed off. Her gait hastened as she walked past the breakfast cabana and instead veered toward the residential suite area. Apparently, she'd lost her appetite for the cup of coffee. That thought sent a tingle of guilt through his center.

Reid rubbed a hand down his face as he watched her walk away. Damn it. What had he just done? He thought about going after her to apologize. Now that he thought about it, he had to admit he'd been less than professional just now. As the newly minted co-owner of the Baja Majestic Resort on the beautiful island of Jamaica, he owed it to all of his guests to treat them well, regardless of any past history. He had no excuse. He'd just been so surprised to see her lying there, the recognition had thrown him off.

But he had to make sure not to slip up like that again. He couldn't forget how important his role was here. No one else was going to get this place up to the standards that the Evanson clientele expected. His father certainly wasn't up to the task. In fact, his father seemed to be doing everything possible to run the family hospitality business into the ground. A gambler through and through, his fraternal parent took way too many chances, risked too many valuables. The cleanup always fell to Reid. This current project being no exception.

He couldn't allow himself to forget how much responsibility he bore. An entire conglomerate of employees, contract workers, and their dependents relied on Evanson Hotels and Resorts for their livelihoods and their future. Not to mention his own parents.

And he'd just gone and insulted a valuable, paying guest.

As much as he hated to admit it, he would have to make up for his behavior. He had to somehow atone for the way he'd just treated Celeste Frajedi.

Merry Christmas, princess.

The derisive words repeatedly echoed through her head as Celeste fled to her deluxe suite and slammed the door behind her. Walking over to the glass screen door leading to the third-floor balcony, she pulled aside the curtains to let the bright sunshine in. He hands were shaking, she realized with no small amount of dismay. He'd rattled her. When was the last time she'd actually felt thrown by a man? Or anyone else, for that matter? Her mother notwithstanding.

Perhaps a better question was why had she let the likes of a pretend Santa Claus in an ill-fitting suit and a side-skewed beard get to her so badly?

There was something about the way he'd looked at her. He clearly hadn't liked what he'd seen. Had her feelings regarding the noisy children been so obvious? She hadn't realized she'd shown any outward signs that she'd been bothered by them but clearly the man had picked up something. He'd called her a scrooge!

Never mind that his labeling of her as such was perilously close to the truth. Still, her attitude to Christmas was none of his business. How dare he treat her the way he had? Her ire and irritation shot up even further as she thought of the derision in his eyes as he'd studied her.

His negative view of her seemed way out of proportion to whatever imagined slight he'd witnessed. It was as if he'd disliked her on sight. Which brought back the question: Why had he seemed so familiar to her?

Celeste shook off the query. The answer hardly mattered. She had no doubt the upper-level management in charge of the resort would be appalled if they knew of the actions of their character actor employee. She was in the very business of appealing to consumers as a professional marketer. The faux Santa's behavior would be considered a nightmare to any business leader. That was no way to treat any customer.

Still, the encounter shouldn't have shaken her up as much as it had. She was a professional, after all. And she'd certainly suffered through worse humiliation. The best thing to do would be to try to just forget about the whole incident and put it completely behind her. She would chalk it up to yet one more instance of a negative holiday memory. As if she needed any more of those.

With a calming inhalation of breath, she sank to the carpeted floor. She would meditate until the whole interaction with the wayward St. Nick was nothing more than a mere ghost of a thought in her head. Relaxing all her muscles, she began to count down from ten. Then she did nothing but clear her mind.

It wasn't easy.

Knock. Knock. Knock.

Celeste had no idea how much time had passed before the annoying knocking roused her out of her deep state of meditative trance. Was it too much to ask for just some calming time after the morning she'd had? Apparently, this day was just going to be one irritation after another.

"Room service," came a soft, feminine voice from the other side of her door.

It took a moment to reorient as Celeste forced herself to stand from her cross-legged sitting position on the floor. Her leg muscles screamed in protest at the abrupt movement as she walked to the door.

"There's been some kind of mistake," she said to the petite uniformed woman standing outside with a cart. "I haven't ordered any room service."

The woman smiled as she shook her head. "This is on the house, madam." Without waiting for acknowledgment, she wheeled the cart toward the center of the room.

"I don't understand?"

The woman's smile didn't falter as she answered. "No charge, madam. Compliments of the resort." She handed her an envelope that had sat in the middle of the tray. With that, she pivoted on her heel and left the room.

Celeste blinked in confusion at the shut door before understanding dawned. Sure enough, when she read the note, her suspicion was confirmed.

Please accept this complimentary gesture as a token of appreciation and regret that

you may have been inconvenienced in any way this morning.
Sincerely, The Baja Majestic Resort.

Someone in upper management must have witnessed the unpleasantness between her and Santa earlier this morning. She studied the goodies before her on the food service cart. They'd certainly made an effort to appease her. A silver carafe of steaming hot coffee sat in the center of the tray. A chilled bottle of champagne sent a curl of frost into the air. Orange juice and a variety of pastries rounded out the offerings. Not bad at all as a conciliatory gesture. Someone was trying hard to make things up to her. A foolish part of her felt guilty that perhaps bad Santa might have been chastised harshly by his superiors. Or even worse, that he'd been fired.

He may have been an overbearing clod, but he didn't deserve to have his livelihood jeopardized. She would have to look into that. The desk attendant in the concierge lounge would surely know exactly what had transpired and the ultimate outcome that had led to the enticing cart she'd just had delivered. A visit later this afternoon wouldn't hurt. If he had been let go, it was probably not too late for her to intervene. Not that he deserved her good will. Still, she would be the bigger person if needed.

It was a role she'd been well groomed for her whole life, after all.

CHAPTER TWO

"ONE OF THE guests would like to see you, *mi paadie.*"

Reid looked up from the spreadsheet he'd been studying to the man who had just entered his office without knocking. Alex was co-owner of the property and Reid felt grateful every day for that fact. He wasn't sure what he would have done without the other man's intimate knowledge of the island and its customs. Not to mention his sharp head for business.

Though Alex definitely had one flaw: a clear aversion to knocking before entering a closed door. Not that Reid had been doing much in the way of concentrating just now. A set of light hazel eyes and tumbling dark hair had interrupted his thoughts unwanted and unbidden throughout the morning. He wondered if she'd liked the tray of goodies he'd had sent to her room. Would she find it all an adequate apology? Or had she huffed in disgust and pushed the tray aside. He suspected the latter. Not that he could really blame her if she had.

"And hello to you too, Alex," he answered his partner without looking away from the screen he hadn't really been focusing on.

"Did you hear what I said, man?"

He nodded. "It appears I'm being summoned by one of the guests, is that it?"

Alex smiled at him. "You wanted to be hands-on, did you not? She's asking for you specifically."

Wasn't it enough that he'd been commandeered into playing Santa this morning when the actor originally hired to play the part had called in sick? The entertainment manager had run to him in a panic. No one else was available to do it. And the resort had announced the event weeks in advance. In the end it was easier just to don the suit and get the whole fiasco over with.

Only he'd come face-to-face with a woman he hadn't ever expected to see again.

Now he apparently had to go smooth the ruffles of a guest who no doubt felt slighted somehow or was trying to finagle a room upgrade.

"I tried to take care of it myself. Explained to her that I was co-owner of the resort. But like I said, the guest insists on seeing you specifically."

Reid sighed and stood. The guest in question had to be one of those checking in this morning who he'd greeted. Apparently, they'd taken it to heart when he'd said that he'd personally see to any detail regarding their stay that they weren't completely happy with. Though why Alex hadn't just taken care of it by partially crediting the guest or explaining that they were at full capacity and had no upgrade to give out was lost on him.

Again, it was probably best to simply go get it over with. It was just clearly going to be one of those days.

Celeste shook her head and tried to blink away the image she was sure she had to be imagining. But when she opened her eyes again, the unwanted vision stood clear as day in front of her still.

This couldn't be happening. "You're the nasty Santa?"

Her words came out harsher and louder than she'd intended. Every eye currently in the concierge lounge turned to stare at her. She distinctly heard a giggle of feminine laughter from behind her somewhere.

To his credit, Reid Evanson looked as shocked as she was at the unexpected turn. Suddenly, the events of the morning seemed to make much more sense. She definitely hadn't been imagining the waves of dislike emanating from the man playing jolly ol' St. Nick.

Well, the feeling went both ways.

"What are you doing here?" she demanded.

He thrust his hands into his pockets before answering. "You're the one who asked for me."

He was being deliberately obtuse. Celeste tried to summon some semblance of calm. It didn't help that the gentleman she'd spoken to earlier was shifting his amused gaze from one of them to the other. None of this was the least bit amusing.

"I mean, what are you doing here on this resort?"

"You two know each other?" the other man wanted to know.

"We were acquainted once," Reid answered briefly.

Despite herself, she found herself studying him. He'd aged well. Clean shaven before, he currently sported a close-cropped beard slightly darker than the sandy blond hair on his head. He wore said hair longer, nearly touching his shoulders. Instead of the Santa suit from earlier, he now wore a formfitting T-shirt tucked into pleated khaki pants. It all showed off the physique of a man who clearly took care of himself. Had he always been so muscular?

"Why did you ask for me?" Reid wanted to know.

"I didn't. I asked to see Santa Claus." This time, the person behind her didn't even bother to try to hide her laughter. Heaven help her, she knew how ridiculous she sounded. She had half a mind to let out a giggle herself.

Without another word, he stepped around the long, highly polished counter and gently took her by the elbow.

"Let's discuss all this in my office."

His office? The room he led her to, if it held human emotions, would have no doubt been insulted to be referred to as such. Floor-to-ceiling glass walls overlooked a scenic beach with a majestic view of the crystal-blue ocean into the horizon. Plush carpeting had her feet sinking in her flip-flops. A grand desk with three large monitors sat in the center of it all.

"You run the resort," she commented as he shut the door behind him.

"I own it. Along with my partner, Alex Wiliston. "He was the gentleman you were speaking with earlier."

The pieces started to fall into place. She remembered now that Reid came from a wealthy family of hoteliers. Though the family business had suffered some losses recently, Reid had taken the helm from his father and turned things around. Last she'd heard, Evanson Properties had not only returned to a profitable enterprise, the company had expanded, all thanks to the prodigal son.

"You decided to expand into the resort business, I take it," Celeste said.

Something flickered behind his eyes. He gave a small nod before answering. "The Caribbean specifically."

"I see. But earlier this morning…when I saw you…" Now she was just rambling.

"Just filling in for an employee who couldn't make it at the last minute."

"I see," she repeated uselessly.

Suddenly, it was all too much. Far from fleeing her unpleasant associations with the holiday as it related to her failed relationship, she'd somehow ended up face-to-face with someone who'd played a major role in the whole fiasco.

Reid had been her ex-fiancé's best man. And she knew he'd never thought her good enough for his buddy.

"Can I get you something to drink?" Reid asked, for lack of anything better to say. How exactly did one proceed with this conversation? The scenario was so completely unexpected in so many myriad ways.

She shook her head. "No. Thank you. I just had

some coffee and a mimosa to wash down several pastries." She took in a shaky breath. "But I'm guessing you already know that. Seeing as you were probably behind the delivery to my room."

"I was. Did you enjoy them?"

Her eyes grew wide. "Are we really doing this?"

"Doing what?"

"Pretending I'm just another one of your regular guests?"

The feeling of guilt from earlier blossomed once again in Reid's chest. Celeste was indeed his guest. A paying customer. He hadn't meant to come off as boorish as he had out on the beach. But he'd just been so thoroughly disconcerted at seeing her again after all this time. If he was being honest with himself, he'd imagined encountering Celeste Frajedi more than a few times over the years. Not that he'd ever been able to explain to himself exactly why that was so. He had no reason to be thinking of her at all.

"But that's exactly what you are," he answered. "An appreciated guest. Hence, my desire to apologize for my behavior earlier. I hope the gesture served as an adequate apology. I should never have let…our history, so to speak…affect in any way how I treat a guest at my establishment. There's no excuse for my having done so," he added with complete sincerity. He really didn't have any kind of excuse. Not even considering the morning he'd had. On top of the missing Santa and the shock of seeing Celeste again, he'd started the day with another aggravating, infuriating phone call with his father, who was once again trying to take over the company he'd almost single-handedly destroyed.

Celeste looked far from convinced by his words.

"I can assure you such behavior on my part won't happen again," he told her. "In fact, you can forget I'm even here."

The skeptical look she speared him with clearly said he hadn't done much to convince her any further.

You can forget I'm even here.

Hah! As if she could forget his presence for even a moment. What a mistake it had been to come here. Of all the resorts she could have chosen as a substitute for her regular vacation spot, how in the world had she landed on this one? The cruel fates were clearly laughing at her.

Celeste flopped herself down on the wide king bed back in her suite and draped an arm across her face. No, she couldn't so easily forget that Reid Evanson was right here on this very island. Nor could she forget the way he'd made her feel three years ago. As if she could never be enough for the likes of his best friend. Never mind that Jack had turned out to be a reckless, disloyal excuse for a fiancé who had eventually left her stranded at the very altar where they were to have made their vows. Sure, now she realized just how much of a favor he'd done her. Aside from saving her from what could have been years of betrayal and heart-break, he'd helped her come to a conclusion about herself. She clearly wasn't the type of woman who was meant for a family or a steady relationship. He'd enabled her to avoid the mistake of a lifetime.

A mistake that could have led her straight down the same path her mother had traveled.

But that knowledge hadn't stopped the sting of rejection, nor the burn of embarrassment as she'd faced down a whole church full of wedding guests to tell them that the ceremony had been suddenly called off.

Reid had been there every step of the way. He'd witnessed her humiliation in its entirety. And she'd received the distinct impression that he felt she'd only gotten what she'd deserved.

An incoming message on her phone pulled her out of her thoughts. The screen lit up with the profile picture of her sister smiling as she held her toddler niece. Celeste groaned and debated whether to answer. On the one hand, she felt drained and conversations with her sister could often be one-sided; Tara's side. On the other hand, Celeste could really use someone to talk to right about now.

With no small amount of doubt, she pressed her thumb on the icon to answer.

"Hey, Tara."

"Hey, sis." The sound of a musical children's show could be heard playing loudly in the background.

"What's up?"

"Just calling to see how things are in paradise. Still can't believe you're there and not here." Ah, so this was the routine guilt-trip call. Cynical as it sounded, Celeste couldn't help the thought given past experience.

Celeste sighed deeply as she shifted to a seated position on the edge of the bed. "Well, it just so happens, I'm beginning to doubt my decision to come."

Tara's sudden exhalation came through loud and clear across the tiny speaker. "What's happened? Spill!"

"Let's just say there's someone here I didn't expect to see. Ever."

"Details, please. Is it a man?"

"Yes, as a matter of fact. But that's not the import—"

But Tara cut her off. "Ooh, this is getting interesting. Is it someone you had a previous fling with? Can you have another one? Hot and heavy with no strings attached! You could so use that, you know."

Celeste rubbed a hand across her tense forehead. Honestly, Tara didn't know her in the least. "I don't do flings."

"Well, maybe you should start. Heaven knows your serious relationships don't turn out so great." She grunted a laugh. "They don't turn out at all."

Ouch. So much for a sisterly conversation to make her feel better. Foolish of her to even entertain the notion. Celeste found herself wondering if she should have answered the phone after all.

"So, who is it?" her sister asked after a heavy pause.

"Never mind. It's not important. Forget I brought it up. How's Mom? And little Nat?"

It wasn't often any of them referred to her niece by her full given name, Natalie.

"They're all fine," Tara answered. But she wasn't having it with the attempted change in topic. "And no way you're going to try to drop the matter of this mystery man. Tell me who you ran into. And tell me what he means to you."

Celeste opened her mouth to respond with a resounding and emphatic denial that Reid Evanson meant absolutely anything to her whatsoever. That she'd hardly thought about him over the past three years.

But the lie wouldn't form on her tongue.

CHAPTER THREE

ALEX STILL STOOD in the middle of Reid's office studying him like a lab specimen. "Is there something I can do for you?" Reid finally asked, ultimately losing the game of visual chicken.

"Yeah. Neither you nor the young lady really answered me earlier when I asked if you two knew each other. It appears you do."

Reid pretended to type on his keyboard. "Then you seem to have answered your own question."

"I have more."

Reid gave up all pretense of trying to get any work done. Leaning back in his leather desk chair, he tried to stretch out some of the tension that seemed to have tied a knot in the back of his neck right at the base of his skull. "Somehow, I knew you would."

"I do. One of them being, exactly how do you know our esteemed guest? I couldn't help but notice she's traveling alone."

"So?"

Alex grinned. "So does that fact have anything to do with you?"

"What? No! Of course not." *Not directly, anyway.*

He hadn't realized he'd mumbled the last part under his breath until Alex questioned him.

"What does that mean, Reid? Not directly?"

Alex sighed, the tension in his neck traveling farther down his spine. He might have to hit the spa later for some kind of back treatment massage. Though he'd been meaning to do that for weeks, ever since he'd arrived at the start of the season.

"It's not what you're thinking, partner."

"Then what is it? You two obviously have some kind of history and not all of it is positive.

Reid almost laughed at that. Less than positive would be an understatement.

"Celeste was almost the wife of a friend of mine. Let's just say he hasn't been the same ever since their relationship ended."

Alex nodded slowly. "Oh. So she dumped him."

Reid rubbed his jaw. "Not exactly."

"Then I don't understand."

Reid ran a hand down his face. He hadn't been sleeping well. There was always something that needed to be done, some detail to attend to. He also had his father's ill-formed takeover attempt to contend with. Now he'd been thrown another curveball in the form of Celeste Frajedi and he wasn't sure how to explain to his partner exactly what had gone down three years ago. It hadn't really had anything to do with him. So it was hard to explain why he'd taken it all so personally back then. Even when it came to explaining it to himself.

"Well, on the surface, Jack was the one who actually did the dumping."

His friend gave him a blank look. "On the surface?"

"She wasn't in the relationship for the right reasons. He told me all about it."

Alex raised an eyebrow.

Reid felt a sensation of discomfort meander down his spine. As if he was betraying a confidence somehow. Though he'd be hard-pressed to identify whose privacy he was uneasy about. Celeste's or Jack's?

"Celeste is a shrewd businesswoman. She's very well known in the industry as one of the most successful marketing executives in New York. The business sites have regular profiles on her. She can be ruthless when she doesn't get what she wants."

"You said your friend hasn't been the same

ever since the disastrous wedding that didn't happen."

Reid nodded. "That's right. He's still traipsing all over Europe, partying in different cities. Living with various women." Some of those women being wealthy, married socialites looking for a good time on the side.

"Huh. And he didn't behave like that before he met Celeste?" Alex wanted to know.

The uneasy feeling grew from tingling sensation to an all-out burning down his back as Reid sought for a truthful way to answer. If he was being completely honest, Jack had always had a propensity to be a bit of a partier, something of a Lothario. If anything, his relationship with Celeste had seemed to temper that side of him.

"It's just different. Trust me. I heard all about it before he called off the wedding. Celeste worked long hours, was never around for him. He said he felt single most of the time."

"Sounds like she's just ambitious."

"I agree that's a commendable trait. But for people like her, it's never enough," Reid answered quickly, though the uneasiness was now sitting like a boulder at the base of his spine. Damn it, why hadn't he scheduled that massage? Maybe they could fit him in between clients.

Alex went on, "She also happens to have booked our most exclusive and pricey deluxe suite for an extended stay. So clearly her ambitions have served her well."

Reid shrugged. "I guess. Again, some people can't seem to have enough." He couldn't even tell anymore if he was talking from personal experience about his father or if he was still referring wholly to Celeste.

"You sound like a man who's only considered one side of a story."

"What's that supposed to mean?"

"You sure you're not confusing cause and effect, partner?"

But his friend didn't give him a chance to answer, just turned and left the office. Apparently, the question was a rhetorical one. Good thing, too. Reid would be hard-pressed to come up with an answer.

Had he been completely unfair in his assessment of Celeste three years ago? Of course, it had occurred to him more than once over the years that he'd only heard one side of the story. But Jack had been his friend since they'd been roommates at university. He was a loyal friend and he'd come through for Reid more than a few times over the years. Reid's father's recklessness and wandering eye had started right around that time, too.

Jack had genuinely seemed shaken when he'd confided in Reid as his nuptials had fast approached. He'd talked about how cold and critical Celeste had suddenly gotten when a couple of Jack's business ventures hadn't panned out. How demanding she'd been that he get back on his feet in all haste.

Reid slammed his laptop shut in frustration.

What did any of it matter now anyhow? It was all past history. Jack had moved on, even if some of his current behavior bordered on self-destructive. He was a grown-up who could make his own choices. Even if everything Jack had told him about her was the absolute truth, Celeste couldn't be faulted for her ex-groom's behavior three years after the fact.

That thought had him feeling like a heel again for the way he'd behaved earlier when he'd first seen her. And also for the assumptions he'd made about her judging him.

In all fairness, Reid had been nothing less than judgmental himself.

Bouncy reggae music greeted her as Celeste made her way down the beach to the seaside cabana she planned to visit for her first dinner here. Her paperback tucked under her arm, she was looking forward to a relaxing evening with a nice glass of wine and a tasty meal of local seafood. Her morning plans had gone woefully astray. The least she deserved right now was a satisfying meal followed by a peaceful stroll on the beach. Then she'd spend the rest of the evening tucked in under her bedcovers, enjoying some further reading. To most women her age, such plans might sound boring and flat. To her, it all sounded like heaven. Exactly what she was looking for during her evening hours on this vacation.

Her step faltered as she approached the cabana. It was already packed and hopping. Every table appeared full. She approached the hostess manning the front entrance.

"Hi, it's just me. Table for one please."

The young lady gave her a sympathetic look before motioning toward the bar area where couples sat sharing various appetizers. Several bartenders stepped around each other mixing drinks and taking orders.

"I'm afraid all we have available right now is bar seating, miss. And those spots are going fast."

Celeste released a sigh of disappointment and made her way to one of the few open bar stools. Squeezing herself in between a burly older man in a Hawaiian shirt and a bikinied brunette, she reached for the drinks menu.

One of the bartenders appeared in front of her within moments. His gold name tag said Phillipe in black lettering. "What can I get for the lovely lady?" He asked her with a wide grin. "And I do mean lovely."

Celeste tried to smile back. He wasn't doing any harm but she really wasn't in any kind of mood for a flirtation. And she had no doubt the young man was flirting. The way he was looking at her left no question about it.

She almost wanted to tell him his efforts were hardly necessary. She always tipped well and if this was sympathy flirting simply because she was sitting at a bar alone in a popular resort, she had no need for it. She placed her order for a glass of sparkling wine and a plate of fish tacos without acknowledging the compliment.

She'd gotten through several pages of her book before her meal arrived.

Phillipe winked at her as he placed the plate in front of her on the bar.

Maybe she should have ordered room service. Now she would have to spend the entire time eating trying to avoid his gaze. And a quick cursory glance in his direction confirmed he was indeed staring at her. Oh, yeah, she couldn't wait to submit an online review about this place after her stay. She'd normally go straight to the owner with her complaints, but he'd been a part of the problem.

Phillipe appeared as soon as she'd taken her last bite. "So, I have a break coming up in a couple of hours. Can I treat you to another drink then?"

She didn't get a chance to answer as a thick baritone voice suddenly sounded from behind her. "Miss Frajedi, I hope you enjoyed your meal."

She didn't need to turn around, recognized the voice immediately as belonging to Reid. Unlike earlier, he wasn't speaking in the low husky voice of a makeshift Santa.

Phillipe immediately took a step back. "Oh. Hey, boss."

Celeste darted a glance over her shoulder. Reid stood only an inch behind her. Arms crossed in front of his chest, his chin tight. He didn't look happy. He merely nodded in a curt acknowledgment of Phillipe's greeting.

Then, to her surprise, he held her hand out to help her up off her stool.

"I haven't settled my bill," she protested.

Reid didn't take his eyes off Phillipe when he answered. "It's on the house."

"Yes, boss," Phillipe immediately responded. She could have sworn he clicked his heels behind the bar.

For lack of anything else to do, Celeste wiped her mouth with her cloth napkin and took Reid's hand before standing. He gently led her away from the crowded bar toward the sand.

"I take it there's a rule about the workers fraternizing with the guests," she ventured after they'd made their way to the beach. The sun was slowly setting across the horizon, throwing brilliant shades of red and orange across the evening sky.

"Not yet, there isn't. Though I've made a mental note to get one drafted ASAP."

His voice sounded strained and tight. If there wasn't any such policy, why did he seem so bothered by Phillipe's behavior? Could it possibly have anything to do with her?

And how many times in one day could she wonder about whether her behavior was going to affect someone else's livelihood, for heaven's sake?

"I'm sorry if you were made to feel uncomfortable during your dinner. We strive to make everyone feel completely at ease at all times. I'll have a word with the staffing manager to make sure it doesn't happen again."

So that was it. She'd been foolish to even feel tempted to look further into it than what lay on the surface.

"Another apology from the top man," she commented, kicking off her sandals to feel the silky soft sand underneath her feet. Reid paused while she nudged them off to the side.

He exhaled. "It appears we are off to a bad start."

She knew he meant the resort, but she took the opportunity to address the proverbial elephant in the room. "Or we're simply continuing along the same path as we were three years ago."

His step didn't falter but she could have sworn she felt him stiffening ever so slightly beside her. "I thought your intention on this trip was to forget all about it."

"Believe me, I see the irony in all of this." An exotic-looking bird flew past them at eye level, a myriad of colors along its wing.

"Tell me something," Celeste began. "You never did appear to be on board with my and Jack's wedding." Or with her, for that matter.

"You didn't seem right for each other," he answered simply.

She couldn't be offended. For he was completely right. Still, his words held enough of a sting that she wondered if she should have even started this conversation.

She could guess what he meant. She and her ex-fiancé were from two different worlds. Celeste had grown up struggling to merely survive while Jack was a trust fund baby who'd always known wealth and privilege.

Much like the man beside her now. Though she'd have to admit, if one were to look closely, the two men didn't really have all that much in common besides factors visible on the surface.

While Reid had worked incredibly hard to make a name for himself in the hospitality business, Jack was a mere figurehead for the yachting company his family owned and operated. Reid had taken all that had been handed to him and then grown and expanded it, becoming an industry titan in the process.

Celeste gave a shake of her head. What good did it do to compare the two men? There was no reason for it. In fact, there was no reason to give Jack another thought. Why had she even brought up his name?

Still, something tugged at her to get to the bottom of Reid's statement, she couldn't seem to help herself. "What do you mean? That we didn't seem right for each other?"

He gave a small shrug. "You're very different personalities. He's not as…ambitious, I guess. You're much more driven. Yet, there's a side of you—" He stopped abruptly. "You know what? Never mind. None of this is my place."

Celeste halted in her tracks and gently nudged him to stop walking. His gaze dropped to where she'd touched him on the elbow. She ignored the way his eyes darkened and quickly dropped her hand. "Please finish what you were going to say. There's a side of me that's what?"

Reid released a deep sigh and looked off into the distance at the horizon. "Just that there's a side of you which must have overwhelmed a man like him. An untamed, stormy quality just underneath your surface. A side a man like Jack wouldn't be able to handle." His eyes seemed to add the words *unlike me*.

Celeste's gasp was audible over the crashing waves behind them. She wouldn't challenge his words, couldn't. For he spoke the very truth. Celeste did everything she could to hide the wild inner-city kid she'd grown up as behind a highly polished professional veneer. She'd made certain to bury the hardscrabble teen who'd bartered, begged and stole simply to survive when the three of them had found themselves homeless on the streets for close to a year.

Then there was her ancestry. She'd fully studied her absent father's Persian roots, intrigued by all she'd learned about the culture. But she'd never explored that part of herself, hadn't so much as looked into visiting that area of the world. Though she'd had plenty of opportunity.

Somehow Reid had seen through all those layers three years ago when they were barely more than strangers.

"I'm not sure how to take what you've just said, Reid," she said once she found her voice again. "That I was somehow too much for Jack to handle."

He turned to fully face her then. "You should take it as a compliment."

Reid had no intention of stopping by the bar when he left his office behind the concierge lounge. He wanted nothing more after a long frustrating day than to head to his suite in the main quarters and pop open a bottle of cabernet and order a thick juicy burger.

But then he'd seen Celeste sitting at the bar by herself. He didn't even want to examine what had made him stop and just watch her for a while. She was alone, but she'd made it clear solitude was what she was after. She'd seemed perfectly content with her book and seafood plate. He'd been ready to move on, get going with the rest of his evening, but then he'd seen the way the bartender had been watching her. He'd found himself moving toward her then. So much for having her forget he was here.

Some strange emotion lodged in his chest when he heard the other man ask to buy her a drink. He didn't even know his intention until he reached her side. And what had possessed him to ask her to walk with him? He probably should have bidden her good-night right after intervening then went about his business. For now, they seemed to be awkwardly strolling along the beach, neither one managing to say anything much by way of conversation after the awkward words about their past.

He shouldn't have told her all the things he'd just shared, didn't even realize he was going to until the words were leaving his mouth.

Celeste cleared her throat. "So, you mentioned you'd recently acquired this place?" She was clearly looking to change the subject.

"Yeah. Last summer. I'd been looking to expand into the Caribbean resort business for a while. Luckily, it was one of the few islands that came through the hurricane season unscathed."

She humphed out a small laugh.

"What?"

"That happens to be the only reason I'm here. My usual spot is in shambles." The faraway look in her eyes told him she missed it. "This was one of the few places left to book."

Reid clapped his hand to his chest in mock offense. "You wound me. You mean to tell me the only reason you chose my resort was for lack of other options?"

She smiled just as a slight breeze blew a dark tendril of hair along her cheek. How silly that his fingers itched to gently tuck it back behind her ear for her.

"I'm afraid so. I rather miss the other place. No offense."

"I'm not so much offended as I am concerned as a business owner. What does it say about this place that you only booked it as a backup?" How many other potential clients were doing the same? The resort could face losing all sorts of business further down the line once the other resorts were back up and running.

"Would you like my professional opinion?"

"Can I afford it?" he teased. "You do have a reputation for being the best."

"Consider this a freebie."

He tilted his head for her to continue. "Well, to put it plainly, your marketing and advertising is somewhat subpar. Frankly, it's garbage. Rubbish."

Double ouch. "Hey, don't get technical now."

She laughed out loud. "Seriously. There's nothing on the website to compel me to click Book Now. Aside from a few pretty pictures of the beach, you don't really say anything very enticing about attractions, nearby landmarks, activities for the guests…"

"Yet you booked it anyway."

"Like I said, I was running out of options and grew concerned everything would sell out. It's competitive enough around Christmas under the best of circumstances. And it's really important to me to get away from the city around the holidays."

He could guess why. It was hard to forget that she and Jack had planned their nuptials around the holiday season. A wedding during Christmas in Manhattan. It was supposed to have been so romantic. Until it had all come crumbling down.

He'd been so quick to take Jack's word for everything and toss the full brunt of responsibility for the mess on her shoulders. Alex's words echoed through his mind. *Are you sure you're not confusing cause and effect, partner?*

Perhaps he had been. All this time.

She continued, bringing his focus back to the matter at hand—his resort's lack of a real media presence that would draw more potential guests. "And I have to be honest, now that I'm here, nothing really compels me to consider returning. Our mutual history aside."

Sighing, he answered her. "You're actually not telling me anything I don't already know. But you have awakened me to the urgency of it all. It's just one more thing on the list. We've been interviewing various marketing firms. None seem to fit the bill."

"If I were you, I would make a decision fairly quick."

She wasn't wrong. The implications of the

failure to do so weren't lost on him. This was all so new. Not for the first time, Reid wondered if he'd bitten off more than he could chew. The differences between running a high-rise hotel in a metropolitan city and running a tropical resort were surprisingly vast.

He'd be even more lost if he didn't have Alex by his side. But clearly it wasn't enough.

"Any suggestions?"

"Are you asking for me to work on my vacation?" she asked, a teasing whimsical tone in her voice.

He couldn't help but laugh. "I'm shameless."

They'd reached the pier that moored the excursion boats. A couple of them were still out, it seemed. He was due to participate in a few of the outings himself, to get a feel for the experiences as the owner. He rested his arms over the steel railing and let his hands dangle over the side. Several blue-gold fish could be seen swimming right under the surface of the water.

"You're absolutely right," he told her. "About communicating better regarding all that we have to offer." The excursions were a prime example. Sure, there were chalkboards and newsletters written up daily detailing the outings available to their guests. But they were only that, mere announcements. Nothing describing the thrilling adventures waiting for those looking for extra experiences, more than just beach volleyball or swim aerobics.

A glimmer of an idea began to form in his head. Reid knew he was too tired and too distracted—a fact that had everything to do with the woman standing next to him—to voice the notion aloud just yet.

But he certainly had some thinking to do. And when he did think it all through, he could only hope Celeste would be on board with his suggestion.

CHAPTER FOUR

CELESTE AWOKE TO the sound of a piece of paper being shuffled under her door.

What the…?

It couldn't be the bill. She wasn't due to check out for several days still. Honestly, if they had confused her with another guest, Reid was going to get an earful about the way his resort was run. A glance at the clock told her it was past nine thirty. That was surprising. She never usually slept this late. But she'd had a restless night. Every time she'd closed her eyes, she'd been met with a set of bright golden ones. Visions of Reid's smile as they walked along the beach. The way he'd glowered at the flirty bartender when he'd approached her after her dinner.

When was the last time she'd taken a walk with a man? She couldn't recall. Had she and Jack visited any beaches? She didn't think so. Probably the reason she preferred to be on a tropical island this time of year.

For that matter, when was the last time she'd simply been with a man? Out on a date? Or in a capacity that wasn't strictly professional? Too long. With groggily heavy limbs, she climbed out of bed, suppressing a groan of frustration. Such thoughts were only going to make her miserable, thinking about all she didn't have in her life.

There's a side of you a man like Jack can't handle.

Celeste shook her head to push thoughts of yesterday's conversation aside.

The item slid under her door turned out to be an envelope with a card inside. Curiouser and curiouser. Her heart thumped in her chest as she removed the card and read its contents.

Please join me for breakfast if you haven't eaten already. I have a few matters I'd like to discuss. It will be worth your time. I'll be in my office until you're ready.
Reid

What in the world could he have in mind? A cry of warning screamed in her head. His cell number was printed on the top half of the card. She should just call him and tell him she had indeed eaten already. Or that she wasn't available. Or just outright tell him she wasn't interested in seeing him or in anything he may have to say.

Though that would be a lie. She was more than intrigued. And more than a little excited at the prospect of seeing him again today. She could hardly get him out of her mind last night. And all the things he'd told her.

As if that wasn't reason enough right there to turn him down.

The man was her ex-fiancé's good friend for heaven's sake. Two short days ago, he practically cornered her on the beach and accused her of being a scrooge. No doubt he still harbored suspicions that she'd ruined her ex's life. After all, what else could he have meant when he'd said she was too much for someone like Jack to handle? Most likely that he thought her too uncultured, too unpolished to sully someone like Jack. Or Reid Evanson, for that matter. Somehow, Reid must have seen straight through her three years ago.

No. There was no reason to go see him.

So why had she walked over to the closet and taken out her prettiest sundress? The red one she knew brought out the hue of her olive skin. With thread-thin straps and a flowy skirt that accented her curves.

The warning cry sounded again, telling her to put the dress back and crawl back into bed if she knew what was good for her.

She lay the dress out on the bureau instead and walked to the shower stall.

* * *

It wouldn't hurt to just ask her, Reid thought as he waited impatiently in his office for Celeste's response to his written invite. He'd long ago given up any pretense of trying to get work done and now just stood staring at the tropical scene before him. A line had formed at the main dining hut for breakfast. He made a mental note to address the wait time in the mornings for food. But his thoughts immediately returned to the woman he'd spent the evening with. He couldn't remember the last time he'd simply walked with a lady along a sandy beach, just talking and enjoying the sunset. He had to admit he'd enjoyed it.

Celeste was already sporting the beginnings of a golden tan, her hair had lightened since the first day she'd arrived. She'd looked like a tempting goddess standing next to him as they stood on the marina pier.

He'd been thinking about her all night.

But none of that had anything to do with his invite asking her to join him for breakfast. That was strictly professional.

The door suddenly flung open and Reid didn't need to look up to know it was Alex. He was the only one who never knocked. "Morning, partner."

Reid merely nodded.

"Your father keeps calling the main office," Alex informed him. "Says you're not returning his calls when he phones you directly."

Reid tried to bridle the surge of irritation that shot through his core. His father. The man was determined to ruin himself at this golden stage of his life. And he'd nearly driven Evanson Properties to the brink of ruin as well until Reid had stepped in and taken over as CEO. All because of a woman. A much younger woman.

Reid rubbed his forehead. "I missed one call from him last night. Not that there's a real need to call him back, in any case. I have no interest in what he has to say."

"Maybe he just wants to talk about his upcoming nuptials."

Reid threw his pen onto his desk. "Ha. If anything, I should be calling my mother about that wedding. Make sure she's all right." His mother had not deserved the way she'd been treated after three decades of marriage to the same man.

"I'll be sure to call him," Reid assured his partner. "Tell him to stop bothering the staff." He made a mental note to reach out to his mother first, however.

Alex gave him a mini salute and turned to leave.

Reid knew exactly why his father was trying to contact him. Now that the company was finally out of the red, Dale Reid was trying desperately to regain the power he'd initially handed over to his only son once the trouble had started.

Which was why he could use Celeste's help. He needed his latest acquisition to be a resounding success. There could be no questioning of his competence or abilities from the board, or anyone else, for that matter. Her marketing expertise could go a long way to establishing this place as a prime vacation spot.

Nope, nothing to do with wanting to see her again. His slight reflection in the glass mocked him even as his brain formed the denial. The truth was, the lines were becoming a bit blurred. Yes, he really was interested in her professional feedback, had no qualms about asking her for it and trying to make some sort of business deal to benefit both of them.

But he couldn't deny he'd been sorely tempted to seek her out this morning even without the business incentive. Something about her called to him, intrigued him like no other woman he'd ever met. The brief time they'd spent together had familiarized him with a woman far different from the one Jack had so often described. "Complained about" would be a more accurate description, though.

He wanted to learn more.

Half an hour after Alex left, a sharp knock on the door had him turning around so swiftly that he sloshed some of the now lukewarm coffee he held onto his desk behind him.

"Come in."

Biting out a curse, he wiped away the spill with the palm of his hand, leaving an unseemly streak of liquid across his highly polished desk. But it was just his office assistant with the latest island tax and duty figures.

He repeated the curse after she'd walked out again. Maybe his invitation had been a mistake. After all, almost an hour had passed.

Looked like Celeste was going to ignore him.

Celeste didn't get a chance to knock on Reid's door before it flung open. In the next moment, she found herself face-to-face with the man himself.

Oomph!

Reid had clearly been in the process of rushing out of the room. He couldn't stop his momentum in time. The crash was unavoidable. She wasn't sure which one of them appeared more taken aback by the collision. A set of strong arms suddenly gripped her around the middle and steadied her back onto her feet before she could topple backward.

"Are you all right?" he asked above her head.

She wasn't sure. Physically she was fine. But a curl of heat seemed to be simmering in the pit of her stomach. The scent of his skin surrounded her, a heady mix of mint, spicy after-shave and pure male. "I'm fine."

"I'm sorry. I wasn't expecting you."

She blinked up at him in confusion. He was the one who had asked her to come see him. But it was hard to think. Her hands itched to reach up and run her fingers through his wavy hair, then move lower and feel the silkiness of his beard. His nearness coupled with her confusion at his words made speaking difficult. "I… uh…got your card."

He had yet to let her go. Heaven help her, she couldn't bring herself to make a move to step out of his embrace. Their faces were inches apart, his breath felt hot against her cheek and lips.

"That was quite a while ago, princess. I wouldn't have pegged you for a late sleeper. Like to linger in bed, do you?"

It wasn't her imagination, his voice had definitely lowered to a huskier, deeper baritone as he uttered the last phrase. But her imagination did rev upward in response. A slew of images flooded her brain. She was in bed in all of them, all right. Only she wasn't alone. And she certainly wasn't sleeping.

His knowing smirk of a smile told her his words had had the intended effect. She shook off the oh-so-dangerous thoughts. What in the world was wrong with her? Two days ago, she would have named Reid Evanson as one the few people on earth she'd be content to never run into again throughout her lifetime. Now, here she was fantasizing about him as he held her in a viselike grip.

"I didn't notice the envelope right away," she lied. What was one small fib in an attempt at saving face? His eyes narrowed on her before traveling down the length of the dress she wore. He wasn't convinced. The truth was she'd agonized over whether to come or not. She'd stood so long in the shower trying to decide, her skin would probably stay pruned into next week.

"I can come back," she managed to say. With some reluctance, she moved out of his arms. He hesitated for the briefest moment before letting her go. "You were obviously on your way out."

"No. Come in," he said then stepped aside, motioning her into the room. "My errand can wait."

Celeste had to take a steadying breath as she moved past him into the spacious office.

"Have you eaten?" he asked as he followed her in. "The offer was to treat you to breakfast, after all."

The answer was no. She hadn't had a bite to eat this morning, just some coffee brewed in the room. But she didn't think she'd be able to summon an appetite right now. Her heart was still stammering in her chest. Her pulse hadn't slowed yet. And she certainly didn't need any more of the strong island coffee in the state she was in.

"Maybe just some tea."

He nodded then fired off a text. Before she'd even had a chance to sit down, a young woman appeared carrying a tray with a steaming carafe and various tea bags.

"Help yourself."

"What did you want to see me about, Reid?" she asked as she poured herself a cup of steaming water and dunked two bags of English breakfast in.

He sat down in the large leather desk chair across from her. The massive mahogany desk between them served as a makeshift barrier and calmed her somewhat. But not completely. Why was she finding herself so affected by this man? She remembered there had always been a strange kind of awareness between them when she'd been engaged to Jack. But she'd chalked it up to conflicting personalities. She certainly hadn't realized all he'd observed about her, the things he'd shared last night.

Reid began to speak. "You mentioned last night that we don't call enough attention to the various activities and attractions that the resort has to offer."

"That's right."

"I know you have no reason to, but I wanted to ask if you'd help me with that."

The successful businesswoman in her suddenly stood at attention. Celeste couldn't deny she was intrigued. "Help you how?"

He shrugged. "It's what you're known for professionally. Developing and running marketing campaigns that appeal to as large a target audience as possible. Tell me how to appeal to potential vacationers about all we have to offer. I'm prepared to pay you for your time. Or, since I'm guessing you don't need the money, I'm willing to offer you a lifetime of free stays with us. As long as we have space, you can come spend a week here completely complimentary."

"I can afford vacations, Reid. Like you said, I don't need the money and I don't need freebie getaways."

"But you have to admit, it would be a nice option to have at your disposal."

His statement reminded her just how far she'd come in life. The girl she'd been, the one who'd grown up with hardly enough to get by let alone the means to travel, would never have believed the opportunity before her now. Hard to believe that girl had grown into the woman who was about to turn such an offer down.

"I'm on vacation. I really wasn't expecting to do any kind of work."

He smiled and tapped a finger against his temple. Had she found that smile so dazzling three years ago when he'd been a member of her wedding party? No wonder she'd done her best to avoid the man. That smile was dangerous. Perhaps she should be avoiding him now, too.

"That's the best part," Reid continued. "What I'm proposing will only enhance your vacation experience."

Now her curiosity was definitely piqued.

"Hear me out," Reid prodded further.

Despite herself, she tilted her head in agreement. What did she have to lose to just listen for a few minutes? Celeste took a sip of the hot, soothing tea then settled in her chair and waited for Reid to begin.

He was perilously close to the verge of babbling nonsensically. Reid knew he wasn't explaining his proposal as well as he could. But it was hard to focus. He still felt Celeste's warmth down the length of his body. The smell of her shampoo lingered in his nose. Her hair was slightly damp, hanging in loose freshly washed waves down her sun-kissed shoulders. She must have come down to see him right after a shower. The sudden, unbidden image of her naked under a stream of steamy water led immediately to yet another much more vivid one. In this next vision, he was under the water with her, running his hands down her skin. Rubbing soapy bubbles over her shoulders and moving his hands lower... That image had him tripping over his words again.

Get a grip.

She was here at his request so that he could run a business proposition by her. He had no business fantasizing about joining her in a steamy shower.

For heaven's sake, he was an accomplished businessman. He had given talks and presentations to world leaders and titans of industry. There was no reason to act so flustered now.

But then again, he had never before imagined anyone in his audiences naked in the shower.

Luckily, Celeste seemed to be getting the gist of what he was trying to say.

She cleared her throat. "Let me get this straight," she began. "You want me to go on the resort's offered excursions, with you. So that I can offer you some suggestions on how to market them to potential guests?"

"Exactly. What do you say? I'd planned to go by myself. But I could use another set of eyes."

"With you?" she repeated, seemingly hung up on that variable. Would she prefer to go by herself? He felt his fists clench at his sides.

"Yes," he answered simply.

"I thought you said you had a business partner?"

"Alex needs to stay here and run things while I'm gone all day. And besides, as someone who lives and grew up on the island, his isn't exactly the vantage point I'm after."

"What kind of excursions are we talking about, exactly?" she asked cautiously. He wasn't surprised that she was trying to ascertain all the details.

"The best Jamaica has to offer. We'd be climbing up a rushing waterfall, visiting a beautiful botanical garden, driving ATV's over some rugged terrain."

Celeste bit her lip. "I'd really intended to just lie on the beach and read for the next several days."

"You're here for what? Over a week? You'll have plenty of opportunity to do so in the coming days."

"How many days exactly are you asking me for?"

"Three, max. We should be able to cover all

the excursions in that amount of time. I've already booked for myself, I'll just add your name."

She held her hands up. "Hold on. I haven't said yes yet."

"But you haven't said no." He paused for effect. "Come on, there are worse ways to spend three days on an island like Jamaica."

It occurred to him that he was trying too hard. With anyone else, he would have laid his offer on the table then walked away. He'd always been known as a tough negotiator, not willing to budge or cajole. For some reason, with Celeste, he was intent on making his case. Not like him at all.

He would have to think about why that was so. After all, this was nothing more than another smart business decision.

Everything he said made perfect sense, Celeste had to admit as she took in exactly what Reid was suggesting. In fact, his proposal was so logical that a small part of her felt a slight tickle of disappointment. Reid was strictly all business at the moment. He was dressed in black slacks this morning, a white button-down shirt accenting the contours of his hardened chest and torso. The shiny gold watch on his wrist caught the sunlight as he gestured with his hands occasionally while speaking.

An appealing, successful, handsome man was asking to spend time with her on various island adventures but his only objective was her business acumen.

That shouldn't have bothered her as much as it did. But that was a silly notion, it wasn't like she and Reid were friends or anything. In fact, a few short days ago, she would have listed him as one of the few people on earth who actually may not even like her.

"Why me?" she asked. There had to be other individuals he could ask. A man like Reid was unlikely to be lacking in female companionship. No doubt he had a girlfriend. Hadn't she just recently stumbled upon a social media posting of Reid accompanying a famous international pop star to some Hollywood gala event? In the photo, he'd had his arm wrapped around her waist as she looked up at him adoringly, clearly smitten. What would *she* think about another woman spending the whole day traipsing around a beautiful island with her man? If their roles were reversed, Celeste didn't think she'd appreciate the circumstances one bit.

Then again, any woman lucky enough to snare Reid was probably more than secure with herself and her status as his girlfriend.

That wayward thought led her to other unwanted ones. She imagined what it would be like to date a man like him. What it would mean if he was sitting here asking her to do these things with her simply because he wanted to spend time with her.

What his lips would feel against hers if he ever were to kiss her.

Dear saints! What in the world was wrong with her? Was it simply because she'd been without a man for so long? Perhaps it was the romantic, exotic location. Something had to be causing such uncharacteristic behavior on her part.

Why hadn't she just said no already? Was she really even entertaining the idea?

She wasn't exactly the outdoors type. Or much of an athlete, for that matter. Sure, she'd scaled countless fences during her youth trying to outrun the latest neighborhood bully after defending her younger sister. And she'd developed some really quick reflexes averting touchy men in city shelters. But that was about the extent of it.

Reid answered her, breaking into the dangerous thoughts. "Think about it. Between your professional credentials and the fact that you take frequent tropical vacations, you're actually the perfect person to accompany me."

Again, nothing but logic behind his reasoning. On the surface, she'd be a fool to turn down such an exciting opportunity; the chance to experience so much more of what the island had to offer and, in the process, acquire a host of memories she'd hold for a lifetime. It was as if he really was Santa and he had just handed her a gift most women would jump at.

Still, she couldn't bring herself to say yes. Not right away.

"I'll need to, Reid. Think about it, that is."

His eyes clouded with disappointment but he gave her a small nod. "As you wish."

She could think of nothing else.

Celeste vowed she would take her time and weigh all the pros and cons before getting back to Reid with her decision. So why did she now find herself in the resort's retail surf shop? Why was she eyeing water shoes that someone would need if she were to go waterfall climbing? And why was there a one-piece swimsuit draped over her arm? She'd only packed two-pieces or tankinis and those wouldn't be terribly conducive to water sports or rock climbing.

So many questions. Like had she imagined it, or had Reid indeed held her just a smidge longer than necessary when they'd collided in his office? That lingering uncertainty was what had her debating the merits of accepting his offer.

Her unexpected attraction to him was throwing her off balance. Reid represented everything in her life that she'd vowed to move on from. He and her ex weren't terribly similar below the surface but they were cut from the same cloth; wealthy, privileged, carefree. They'd been life-long friends, for heaven's sake.

Reid may be a successful hospitality indus-try tycoon but men like him didn't understand women like her. They didn't get what it took to succeed in life when you'd literally started with nothing. Or what it was like to try to hold a near full-time job during high school and still main-tain your grades well enough. Or when your sin-gle parent couldn't earn enough to make ends meet, which meant that you and your younger sister often went hungry. Or without adequate shelter.

None of that however had anything to do with the matter at hand currently. She couldn't keep Reid waiting for long.

A sales clerk approached her from across the aisle. The young woman had a dazzling smile and long, tight braids cascading down her back.

"Can I be of assistance, miss?"

Celeste returned her smile. "I'm just being indecisive, that's all." In so many ways.

She pointed to the water shoes Celeste held. "Well, if you're going on the tour tomorrow to climb Dunn's River, you'll need sturdier protection than those for your feet."

That was indeed one of the excursions Reid had asked her to attend.

"Follow me," the clerk said, then turned to lead her to a different shelf. "These are a bit thicker in the sole. Better to grip the slippery rocks."

Just how slippery were those rocks? Maybe this was a sign. The universe had sent this pretty sales clerk to warn her not to try to do anything so perilous as climbing up a waterfall. She liked to think she was fit. But her exercise regimen mainly consisted of meditation and yoga. Though the latter could be strenuous and muscle straining, Celeste was no rock climber.

The sales clerk suddenly laughed. "You look very concerned."

"I am a bit," Celeste admitted. "I've never climbed up a waterfall before."

"Trust me, you will love it. It's an experience of a lifetime. There are professional, knowledgeable guides to help you every step of the way. You'll do fine."

"I'm not so sure. Sounds like it could be very dangerous." Part of her was referring to so much more than the climb. She'd be opening herself up to danger on so many other fronts. She could no longer deny her attraction to her ex-fiancé's best man. An attraction which was wrong on so many levels.

The more Jack had learned about her background, the more distant he'd grown. Ultimately, he'd walked away.

What made her think Reid would be any different?

"This isn't an opportunity you want to miss. What if you never get the chance again?" the smiling clerk asked, breaking into her thoughts.

That was certainly something to consider.

"It's just not an activity I would normally do," Celeste admitted.

The woman's smile grew. "What better time than on vacation to take a chance and try something new?"

Celeste didn't bother to explain. She wasn't usually the type to take chances. Too many things could go wrong. Life ran so much smoother when every detail was attended to and risky endeavors were steadfastly avoided. The only time she'd been remiss in that regard had resulted in humiliation and heartbreak.

Climbing up some slippery rocks as a waterfall cascaded over your body certainly wasn't on the same scale as agreeing to marry a man you had many reservations about. But still, risk was risk. What would happen to her mother if anything were to happen to Celeste? Or to her sister and young niece, for that matter? She knew they'd be taken care of financially, she'd seen to that years ago. But they needed her so much more than just monetarily.

Then again, maybe she was just flattering herself. Maybe Tara and her mom would figure out how to move forward without her, especially as long as the checks kept on coming.

Plus, how dangerous could these excursions really be? It wasn't like she was putting her life in danger. From what Reid had explained, dozens of tourists a day participated in this particular activity. Even young children.

She'd spent countless days on vacation lying on lounge chairs with her nose in the pages of a book. Maybe it was time to try something different.

"Also," the clerk continued, "your man is going to love the way you look in that." She pointed to the swimsuit Celeste held. "That shade of blue will look great with your skin tone and dark hair."

"Oh! I'm not— I mean, we don't—"

The other woman quirked an eyebrow at her. "Are you going alone? That's all right, too. Many people do."

"No. I won't be alone. I am going with a man. It's just that—well, he isn't *my* man. Just a man, you see. And we're not even going as friends. Not really. It's more a business thing."

For Pete's sake. Now she was just a rambling, incoherent mess. Hard to believe she made her living the way she did.

Not surprisingly, the clerk stood staring at her with a look of utter confusion on her face.

"You'll be climbing the falls for business?" she asked.

Celeste nodded. "Something like that. It's hard to explain."

"I see."

She lifted the items in her arms and gestured to the shoes the clerk held. "I'd like to charge these to the room, please."

There it was. Somehow, without even realizing, it appeared she'd come to a decision after all.

She could only hope she wouldn't regret it.

CHAPTER FIVE

HER PHONE VIBRATED in her dress pocket just as Celeste slid her keycard into the door lock slot. So much for giving her time to get back to him. Assuming it had to be Reid, she fished it out of her pocket and clicked before checking to be sure.

She was mistaken. It was her mother's voice that greeted her on the other end.

"Are you on the beach, enjoying some fruity frou-frou drink with a paper umbrella?" The question was asked in a mean-spirited and mocking tone.

Celeste took a fortifying breath. The way her mother's words slurred and rolled into one another gave all the indications that she was the one indulging in drink at the moment. And Wendy's choice of beverage would never be described as frou-frou. Conversations with her mother were always beyond draining under the best of circumstances. When she was drinking, they bordered on traumatic.

Though she could be a caring and nurturing parent when sober, Wendy Frajedi was a mean drunk.

"Hello, Mother. I just walked into my room after picking up some things from the resort shop, as a matter of fact."

"Huh. Must be nice. Do you know how much I need around the house? If only I had a daughter who was willing to help out with some shopping for me." Wendy put extra emphasis on the last word.

Celeste pinched the bridge of her nose and kicked the door shut behind her. "I left a sizable amount of cash in the jar last time I was there, Mom."

"That doesn't mean you're around to help me shop and put the stuff away now, does it?"

She wanted to tell her parent that she was perfectly capable of getting her own groceries or whatever else might be needed. But opposing her mother in any way when she was like this only led to long, drawn-out arguments that merely served to frustrate and demoralize her, sometimes to the brink of tears. As much as she hated to admit it, Wendy Frajedi was the one person on the planet who could make her feel like she hadn't done anything right in her life, even when she knew it was 99 percent the vodka talking.

It was just that the 1 percent delivered a mountain of hurt.

Celeste had long ago given up trying push back when her mother was in her cups. The tension only escalated if she did so. No. Her mom would have to get off her chest all that she felt compelled to say. Then she would sleep off the bender until a pounding hangover headache woke her up. At which point a different kind of misery would befall her. The woman refused treatment as she insisted she didn't have a problem, that she only drank once in a while.

"How come you never invite me or your sister on some fancy-schmancy vacation?" Wendy now demanded to know.

Like déjà vu. The two of them went through this every year. More accurately, they went through it every time Celeste traveled. "You know you don't like airplanes, Mom. Tara can hardly be expected to travel with the baby. And last year she was pregnant."

Her mother grunted in disgust at her response. "There are plenty of places we can drive to together, aren't there?"

Celeste couldn't think of anything less relaxing than driving long-distance with her sibling and parent in order to spend several days together. Of course, she didn't bother to say so.

"I needed to get away, Mom. I'll make it up to you."

Her mother's peal of laughter screeched loudly into the phone. "Yeah, right. Like I'd believe that."

"Is there somewhere specific you'd like to visit?" Celeste threw out the question, just to play devil's advocate. Her mother had no real desire to travel. Right now, she just wanted to chastise her daughter for doing so.

"How should I know? You're the smarty pants in the family."

And her mother would never forgive her for being smart. Or driven. Or successful. She would never understand her older child's fierce desire to escape the cloud of destitution their family had been born under. Celeste sighed. Her mother usually took longer to get to this point in the conversation. Next would come the tirade; the outlining of all the things that were wrong with Wendy's life and how impossible it was to better any of it.

"I'm a little too old to be watching that baby, you know," her mother began, describing Tara's nine-month-old daughter. Her only grandchild. "Since you're not around, I've had to do it more times than I'd like to think."

Celeste didn't bother to remind her mother that she'd only been gone for about three days.

Wendy couldn't have babysat more than once or twice since then.

But logic wasn't the point of these conversations. "Sorry, Mother. How is little Nat?" she asked in an attempt to change the subject.

"Loud. Cries a lot. Must be teething or somethin'. I tell ya, I couldn't wait to get outta there."

Celeste bit back the surge of anger that suddenly rose to the surface. Tara's daughter was the sweetest, most loving baby, despite the lineage of women she came from. Celeste uttered a prayer to heaven at least once a day that the pleasant nature the child had been born with somehow carried through as she grew up. She'd do everything she could to ensure that happened.

One thing was for certain, Celeste would have to arrange for a professional babysitter for the child the next time she traveled. She might even have to look into hiring one now long-distance. She didn't want Wendy around the child if she was growing resentful of the responsibility. Celeste was completely confident that Wendy wouldn't drink around the baby. She preferred to drink alone in the privacy of her own apartment, without judging eyes advising her to slow down or stop.

But it simply wasn't worth the risk.

Celeste made a mental note to look into a sitter first thing tomorrow morning and tell Tara.

But Wendy's next words made the issue a moot one. "Thank goodness I won't have to watch her anymore. Not anytime soon. Looks like your sister was let go again."

Celeste didn't even know why she was surprised. It was a wonder her sister ever got hired at all. She tended to arrive late to work and then slacked off once she got there. No doubt Tara's latest setback had something of a hand in her mother's afternoon of binge drinking.

"That was her third job this year, wasn't it?"

Her mother pounced. "Well, I guess we can't all be as perfect as you." Bingo. Her mother had now hit all the usual notes. Celeste hoped she felt some semblance of relief now that it was out of her system. For the moment and until next time.

Celeste resisted the urge to ask her outright. *Feel better now, Mom?*

Sadly enough, the answer was still no. And Wendy would feel awful once she woke up and remembered how she'd spoken to her eldest daughter. Then the barrage of apologies would start.

Until it all happened again.

* * *

By the time he'd walked the entirety of the resort for the third time, Reid had to admit that he was trying to seek Celeste out. It galled him that she hadn't responded yet to his proposal.

He also had to admit that he'd be profoundly disappointed if she ultimately turned him down. Which was sort of funny if one thought about it. Before he'd laid eyes on her, he had a determined set plan in place to attend the excursions by himself and then meet with a marketing team to see how best to advertise them. Now, the thought of going by himself held absolutely zero appeal.

He was doing this for the sake of expanding resort bookings. He wanted this place to be the first resort people thought of when they decided to vacation in Jamaica. Celeste could really help him toward that goal. That was the only purpose behind him asking her to accompany him.

So why did a surge of pleasure shoot through his chest when he finally did spot her? Until he approached, that is. The closer he got to where she sat, the more he could see something was wrong.

She sat alone at a tall table at the outdoor pub by the stage. A plate of French fries sat untouched in front of her. She was staring at the glass she held which must have once been a frozen drink but now appeared to be a mixture of icy slush and dark rum.

An unfamiliar sensation of concern settled in his gut.

"Something wrong with the fries? Do I have to speak to the chefs?"

She blinked up at him in confusion, holding her hand to her forehead to block the sun in her eyes. "Reid." She gave him a smile that didn't seem quite genuine enough to reach her eyes.

"Were the fries not done to your liking?"

She looked down at her plate in surprise, as if she'd forgotten it was there. Maybe she had. She'd certainly been deep in thought when he'd approached her.

"I guess I wasn't all that hungry."

"May I?" he gestured to the other empty stool at her high top table.

"By all means."

She began to speak as soon as he sat down. "I know I still owe you an answer."

It surprised him that her failure to respond to his proposal was the furthest thing from his mind at the moment. His first concern was why she appeared so, well, sad.

"This is going to sound like the worst kind of pickup line, but…" he hesitated. Maybe probing would be overstepping his bounds.

"Yes?"

"It really is such a shame to look so down on such a beautiful day in paradise."

She let out a small laugh. "You're right. That does sound like a bad pickup line. And here I thought you would have a better game. Given your reputation as such a player and all."

He laughed in return, ducked his head in mock embarrassment. "I might be out of practice. I've been a little busy with this place."

"Fair enough."

What little there was of the smile on her face faltered then disappeared completely.

"Is everything all right?" he asked, now downright worried for her.

"Just fine." He definitely didn't believe her. Was debating whether to push when she spoke again. "And I'd like to say yes, by the way."

For the briefest moment, he wasn't sure what she was referring to. Then understanding dawned. She was agreeing to help him with the marketing ideas.

But right now, all he felt was concern. Celeste looked far from a woman on vacation. Rather, she looked forlorn and melancholy.

Not that it was any of his business.

"Did you hear me?" she asked.

He summoned a pleased grin. "Glad to hear

it. You won't regret this. Let's shake on it," he suggested, holding out his hand.

Her hand felt small and dainty in his large palm. He could probably wrap his thumb and forefinger around her tiny wrist. It occurred to him just how vulnerable she looked. Formidable businesswoman or not, Celeste Frajedi had a softness about her that set his protective instincts at high guard status. As backward and downright Neanderthal as that sounded.

He wondered if a man was behind her current state of sadness. That thought had him reeling with an unreasonable degree of anger. She'd been hurt enough romantically for one lifetime.

Celeste had so much going for her. Any man would be a fool to treat her poorly in any way. How shameful that he hadn't seen that three years ago. Something had blinded him then to Jack's faults.

He'd been told more than once that he could be loyal to a fault. Next time he and Jack crossed paths, he would have a few words he'd like to share with the other man.

Not that it would be any time soon. The two of them had certainly grown apart since the ill-fated wedding. Reid couldn't even recall the last time the two of them had spoken to each other live. For all he knew, Celeste and Jack were still in touch. Maybe Jack was the reason for her current state of sorrow. He felt his neck muscles tighten at the thought. After all, the last time he'd witnessed such sorrow on her face, Jack had been the precise cause.

Without thinking, he blurted out the pesky question that had been lurking in his brain. "So, what exactly went down that day?"

Celeste didn't even pretend to not know what he was referring to.

Her lips tightened into an ironic smile. "You'd like to ask me about my failed wedding. Now of all times."

He wasn't sure what that last part meant, decided to push on anyway. "Only if you'd like to talk about it." She certainly appeared as if she could use the excuse to get something off her mind.

"You said yourself that he and I seemed to be incompatible. Turns out you were right. As I'm sure you heard from the man himself."

"I'd like to hear your take on it," he prompted.

She shrugged ever so slightly, trailed a finger over the condensation down the side of her glass before she finally spoke. "Jack gave me a final ultimatum as a test. And I failed miserably."

Celeste couldn't bring herself to look up away from her glass. But she could feel Reid's questioning eyes on her nevertheless. He remained silent at her cryptic remark, simply waited for her to continue. But she'd be hard pressed to decide exactly where to begin. The troublesome signs that her engagement was doomed had grown more and more frequent as the wedding day had approached. She'd just chosen to ignore them.

"What kind of test?" Reid wanted to know.

This was all so difficult to talk about, Celeste thought. She'd done her best to try to put it all behind her. To try to forget. What kind of woman was left behind at the altar? How could she ever trust in her feelings again when she'd fallen for a man who had been cruel enough to do such a thing?

Visions of that nightmarish day flooded her brain. Her coworkers seated in the pews, her friends from school, various other invitees. All of them giving her looks of unmitigated pity. The disappointment flooding her mother's face. She'd never felt such a strong desire to sink into the floor and disappear. There'd been no father to walk her down the aisle. Celeste had asked a former mentor to do her the honor. The look on the man's face as they'd waited and waited for a groom who'd never appeared had nearly crushed her soul. Bless him, he'd been the one to finally make the announcement as she'd fled, trying to squelch the flood of tears before she could get away. She'd vowed never to give her heart to another man unless she was absolutely sure of his love and commitment.

"Celeste? What kind of test?" Reid repeated.

She forced herself to shake off the thoughts. "A week before the wedding, Jack decided he wanted to elope."

Reid's eyebrows lifted in surprise. She'd always wondered if Reid had been in on the idea as best man. His reaction just now made it clear he hadn't been.

"I see," Reid answered, clearly confused.

He didn't really. And there was no way to explain it to him, Celeste thought. Jack's sudden decision to forgo a traditional ceremony had had nothing to do with wanting a private event between the two of them.

It had everything to do with being embarrassed in front of his friends and loved ones about the kind of family she came from. Eloping would keep Tara and her mother out of sight. The love Jack supposedly felt for her wasn't enough to overcome the shame he felt about her family.

She'd called his bluff. And he'd walked away.

"I take it you weren't keen on the idea," Reid said.

She shrugged. "I wanted a traditional wedding," she answered simply, leaving out the more relevant part—mainly that her fiancé had been too much of a snob to accept her for who she was and where she came from. In hindsight, Jack's strategy was all too clear. He'd wanted a cowardly way out of marrying her. So he'd given her a choice that wasn't really a choice. How could she have turned her back on the two most important people in her life on the biggest day of her life?

Reid's expression held every indication that he suspected there was far more to the story than she was telling. Well, this was as much as she was willing to divulge. As much as her heart could take to reveal.

"I've known Jack for most of my life," Reid finally spoke after a long bout of silence, one where she couldn't quite meet his questioning gaze. "I've seen him act downright reckless all too often." He paused to take a deep breath and looked away off to the side. "But losing you has to be the most foolish thing he's ever done."

His words hung heavy and loaded in the air. Reid watched as Celeste's eyes grew wide. He didn't regret what he'd just said, but decided not to push the conversation any further. Celeste also appeared to have said all she was willing to say. For now.

She slowly pushed her glass away before standing. "Now that that's all out of the way, I should go back to my room and try to get an early night. I'm guessing we have quite the day ahead of us tomorrow. It won't do for me to be tired and sluggish."

Reid gently grasped her arm. "I have a better idea."

Her gaze dropped to where he touched her. For the briefest moment, neither one of them moved. Electricity seemed to crackle through the early evening air.

Finally, Celeste slowly sat back down and broke the silence. "What would that be?"

He motioned to her full plate. "Well, you clearly haven't eaten. We'll have to remedy that. Aside from not being tired tomorrow, we can't have you malnourished."

"Hardly a danger, but what did you have in mind?"

"Dinner to start with?"

Her eyebrows lifted in question. "Just to start? What then?"

He couldn't help but grin. "It happens to be Thursday."

"So?"

"Don't you read the daily newsletter? Thursdays are karaoke nights on the beach. Tonight's theme is Christmas carols."

Celeste's spine stiffened. "I don't think that's really—"

But he stopped her. "Karaoke happens to be one of the activities we'd like to highlight when advertising. We had a deal that you just agreed to, remember?"

Her look of horror told him she wanted badly to forget.

She really needed to head this development off at the pass. The steely set of determination in Reid's eyes only upped her panic. He couldn't possibly see her as a karaoke kind of gal in any way, shape, or form.

"Uh. I don't do public singing. And I certainly don't do Christmas carols."

He shook his head real slow. "This is all about you experiencing everything the Baja Majestic has to offer. That includes karaoke."

Celeste rubbed a weary hand across her forehead. What had she gotten herself into here? "Listen, I don't so much as sing in the shower."

Something darkened behind his gaze at her words. "I'm certainly not going to do it in front of a beach full of strangers," she added.

Reid glanced at his shiny, expensive watch. She'd been speculating that it was a Rolex. "There's plenty of time to discuss it. Let's go get some real food." He picked up a fry and popped it in his mouth even as he declared her discarded snack fake.

"There's nothing to discuss, Reid."

He stood and took her by the elbow, nudging her to join him. "Sure there is. First, we figure out dinner. Hibachi's always good. My favorite chef's on tonight. Or we could do the Mediterranean restaurant. The kebabs melt in your mouth. Something to do with the marinade."

She wanted to deny that she was hungry, but her stomach had other plans. An audible rumble sounded from her midsection when he mentioned the word kebab.

Reid let out a short but hearty laugh. "Mediterranean it is. Let's go."

He didn't give her a chance to argue. A few minutes later, they were climbing a spiral cement staircase to a building fashioned to appear like an ancient Greek cathedral complete with Ionic columns and goddess statues. The petite blonde maître d' approached them as soon as they entered. Her eyes lit up as she greeted Reid. Her crush was nearly visible. Not that she could be blamed for it.

"Hey, boss. You haven't been in for a while."

Reid returned her smile with a much more platonic one.

"My friend here would like to try the kebab, Michelle. Table for two please."

Michelle spared a glance in her direction, clearly appraising. She wondered if she passed some sort of Reid-worthy test as far as the other woman was concerned. Probably not.

"Of course, right this way."

They were seated at an elegant table with ivory-white table settings, a crisply laundered tablecloth, and tall lit candles. All in all, the atmosphere in the dining area could only be described as highly romantic. That notion frayed her nerves a bit further. She absolutely could not be having any thoughts of romance whatsoever. Despite how much she'd shared of herself with Reid earlier. He'd simply caught her at a vulnerable moment. Phone calls with her mother when she was drunk tended to bring out that vulnerability.

She forced herself to focus on the menu. Every entrée and salad description made her mouth water. To think, she'd been convinced she wasn't hungry at first. But the aroma of spices in the air combined with what she read on the menu had her stomach grumbling once more. How very ladylike. Good heavens, it hadn't been that long since she'd enjoyed male companionship. Why was she coming off as such an awkward neophyte?

A white-jacketed waiter took their order within minutes. Clearly, every worker in the restaurant had been made aware that the co-owner was in attendance. Another waiter soon appeared and placed a small glass jug with clear liquid in the center of the table.

Celeste stared at it in confusion. "Is that all the water we're getting?"

Reid looked up from his menu. "Darling, that's not water. And if you're not familiar with it, I would definitely not drink it as if it were."

It was hard not to react internally to the endearment. Reid hadn't really meant anything with the affectionate word, but something curled deep in her belly nonetheless.

She figured out what he was getting at as far as the small pitcher was concerned. Greek architecture, Mediterranean cuisine. "It's ouzo, isn't it?"

"That it is. I'm guessing you've never had it?"

"Never," she answered. "And I probably shouldn't start today."

He nodded. "It's potent stuff. If you change your mind, start with a really small sip. Or we could have it watered down for you."

She shook her head. The last thing she needed in his presence was anything else throwing her off balance in any way. She felt enough out of her element as it was.

"I'll stick to the simple white wine, thanks."

He ordered her a chardonnay then poured

himself a small amount of the ouzo into a shot glass that the waiter returned with. By the time their food arrived, the crisp, fruity wine had done a great deal to smooth her frazzled nerves. Between the disastrous phone call with her mother and the sheer magnitude of Reid's presence, she found it rather surprising that she was finally starting to relax.

Until Reid brought up the matter of karaoke again.

"I just thought you were a woman open to trying new things." He was clearly goading her. Unfortunately, she fell for the trap. In a way she was too tipsy to realize she'd quickly regret.

"I am about certain things. See, look."

Reaching for the remaining sliver of ouzo that sat in the mini pitcher. It was barely more than half a tablespoon. How strong could it be? She downed it in one swift gulp. Then gasped in shock as liquid fire shot through her midsection.

Reid sat staring at her wide-eyed. What had possessed her to do something so reckless? Suddenly, he threw his head back and barked out in laughter. He then gave a mini seated salute.

"I'm gonna need some more water."

Her belly felt like she'd swallowed a lit match. A rush of heat shot through to her cheeks. The room seemed to have tilted slightly. None of that was particularly funny.

So she wasn't quite sure why she returned Reid's laugh with a hearty one of her own.

Reid had stopped speculating what might have led to the scene he'd come across earlier this evening when he'd found Celeste so forlorn and defeated at the outside pub. But there was no question she seemed to be enjoying herself now. If her wide smile was any indication.

A trove of pleasure blossomed in his chest at the thought that he'd helped put that smile on her face. As they left the restaurant and headed toward the beach, he took the opportunity to study her, the way he had through most of dinner.

She was unlike anyone he'd ever met. How could Jack have ever described her as standoffish and guarded? No doubt she'd tried to present herself that way in response to Jack's stilted demeanor.

He wished he'd bothered to ask three years ago. Maybe he could have talked some sense into his friend. Then again, he wouldn't be sitting with her here now if he'd done so. Selfish or not, he didn't feel sorry that the turn of events had led to this current moment.

"How do you feel?" he asked as they reached the sand.

"Surprisingly all right. But I don't think I'll be looking to do any more shots of ouzo this evening. Or ever again," she added after the slightest pause.

"Probably a wise decision."

A speaker suddenly sounded from near the water with a bouncy rendition of "Holly Jolly Christmas."

"We're headed to the karaoke event, aren't we?" she asked, a note of resignation laced in her voice.

"Trust me, you don't want to miss it."

She sighed and continued walking. "I suppose it can't hurt to watch for a bit. There are worse ways to spend the evening."

Reid hung his head low in mock offense. "Wow, not the most enthusiastic response I've gotten to the prospect of spending time with me, but I guess I'll take it."

"Trust me, it's nothing less than a compliment. I can't think of one other person who could convince me to go near an event featuring amateur singing of Christmas carols."

There was no reason for her comment to cause the rush of pleasure in him that it did.

"You sure it's me? It might be the ouzo," he teased.

She groaned out loud. "I can't believe I did that."

They'd reached the area by the wooden stage, the music growing louder by the second. The slow crashing of the waves behind them grew more and more muted. An impressive crowd had gathered. Two staffers sat at a table, surrounded by laptops and sound equipment. They each had Santa hats on. Another staffer dressed as an elf walked around passing out the same hats to guests.

Reid realized he was taking it all in more as a participant rather than the co-owner of the resort. He couldn't recall when that had ever happened before on one of his properties. He risked a glance at the woman next to him. She had to be the reason he was suddenly viewing things through different eyes. Though for the life of him he wouldn't be able to explain why. What manner of effect did she have on him?

"Mr. Evanson," the hat deliverer had reached them. Without asking, she reached up and placed one atop his head. Then she turned and did the same to Celeste.

Reid noticed her hat was different. It had a floral design instead of plain white at the base. The lettering said You've Been Chosen.

The hat elf clapped her hands. "You've been chosen, madam!"

Celeste blinked at her in confusion. She looked at him for some clarity. Damned if he knew what was going on.

"Chosen?"

"You have one of the special hats," the elf answered.

"Special how?"

"It's our version of mistletoe. But you have a choice. You can perform a song onstage."

Celeste's hand flew to her mouth in horror. "What's the other option?"

The elf laughed in response. "You kiss someone, silly. That's how mistletoe works, right?"

The staffer looked pointedly at Reid as she explained. Her coworkers had all turned their focus on the three of them. Several of the revelers turned to watch, as well. So, his employees were taking the opportunity to have a little fun at their boss's expense. Nothing malicious, he knew. Harmless fun.

But Celeste looked as if she'd swallowed a raw conch.

He discreetly drew the staffer's attention and gave a slight, almost imperceptible shake of his head. *Drop it.*

The elf immediately nodded in agreement. But it was too late. The crowd had now gotten involved. Chants of encouragement had begun.

"I'm not up for either of those options," Celeste said in a low voice. Enough of the crowd heard her that the encouraging cheers started to switch to long, exaggerated boos.

This was his fault, Reid thought as he tried

to find the quickest path out of the crowd. He'd never forgive himself if she was humiliated.

"Come on," a man urged her to their left. "Pick one."

Reid clenched his hand by his side. His fingers itched to shove the man aside and away from her but it wouldn't do to accost one of his guests.

He grabbed Celeste by the wrist and began to lead her away. The boos grew louder.

She surprised him by halting them both to a stop. When he turned in question, she'd gone pale.

"It's okay. I'll do it," she declared, breathless, her voice aquiver.

He pivoted to face her fully. "You don't have to, Celeste. I'll get you out of here," he said on a low whisper against her ear so that only she could hear.

She nodded slowly. "I'm sure. I don't run from things," she offered with a shaky smile. "Then again, that might just be the ouzo talking."

Without waiting for his response, she turned toward the stage and stepped toward it. Reid shook off his shock and quickly followed her up the steps onto the platform.

The crowd erupted in cheers and applause once more. Reid placed his hand gently on her waist at the base of her spine. Bowing slightly to the crowd, he took the mike.

"What are you doing?" Celeste asked him.

He shrugged. "Can't let you have all the fun, can I? What are we singing?"

CHAPTER SIX

IF SHE HAD somehow managed to sing in front of a throng of beach partygoers last night, the task before her should be a piece of cake.

Celeste took Reid's hand as he helped her off the charter boat onto the smooth beach they'd spent half an hour sailing to after leaving the Baja Majestic earlier this morning.

She could do this. Besides, part of her was looking forward to it maybe just a little. The waterfall they were to climb up couldn't be that tall, could it? She got her answer soon enough.

The falls was tall, all right. But it didn't seem terribly steep. She took a steadying breath, reminding herself that she'd signed up for this. There would be no backing out now. Just like last night onstage.

Hard to believe but she felt a quiver of a smile tug her lips at the memory. She and Reid had butchered "Jingle Bells" so badly, it was a wonder they hadn't been escorted off stage. To think she could laugh about it now, when at the time she'd thought she might faint with nervousness. What choice had she had? She wasn't going to hightail it and run away in front of all those people. And what was the other option? To kiss Reid.

She'd thought about it, she really had. In fact, she'd found herself oh-so-tempted to just lean into him, even in front of all those people, and find out once and for all what his lips would taste like, how they would feel up against her own.

Singing in front of strangers had absolutely been the safer choice.

Though *singing* might be too generous a word. Reid had stayed onstage with her and "sung" too.

"You ready?" he asked her now.

"I suppose." She followed him to the base where two guides were waiting for them. After a brief summary of safety measures and what to expect, they began the climb by stepping on the first big boulder.

So far so good.

Granted, it was literally the first step. But she'd take any encouragement where she could get it. They were both absolutely soaked in no time. Reid seemed unfazed by the sheer physicality required. Lithe and agile, she got the feeling he'd be bounding upward boulder to boulder if he wasn't hampered by her. Despite the early-morning heat, there was enough of a breeze and shaded areas that she found herself shivering with cold.

In response, Reid rubbed his palms absent-mindedly over her arms when they came to a brief stop before scaling the next large boulder. More than once, she lost her footing on the slippery rocks and he was there to catch and steady her. She'd always prided herself on her independence. Even after her broken engagement, Celeste defined herself by her own successes, for being her own person. But something about the way Reid kept rescuing her from slips and falls awakened a side of her she didn't recognize. It was nice for once to literally have someone to fall back on.

The noise of the gushing water made conversation impossible. Not that she would have known what to say. His touch sent electricity over her skin.

Forty-five minutes later, they'd finally reached the top. Her muscles quivered with exhaustion. But that wasn't all she felt. She was elated. She'd done it. She'd conquered the phenomenal task—to her, anyway—of climbing up a one-hundred-and-fifty-foot waterfall.

Their guides congratulated them with a round

of high fives. Reid reached for his waterproof wallet and handed several wilted bills to the two men.

He turned to her with a wide grin. "You did it!"

She didn't get a chance to respond as he lifted her by the waist and twirled her around in a tight embrace.

Celeste didn't even bother to try to suppress her squeal of laughter. She *had* done it! She'd successfully conquered a feat she wouldn't have even attempted a week ago. All because Reid was by her side throughout it all.

She would have to examine at some point what that meant for her going forward. But right now, she was due a bit of a celebration.

When he sat her back on her feet, an unknown heaviness hung in the air between them. She could have sworn he was going to touch her again. Instead, he clenched his hands into tight fists and squeezed his eyes shut.

Heavens. Maybe she should have asked for that kiss last night when she'd had an excuse.

"Reid?" she wasn't even sure what she was asking of him. Just then, another couple cleared the top of the waterfall and ran past them laughing. Several feet away, they stopped to embrace and indulge in a long and ardent kiss. A stab of longing hit Celeste deep in her core and she couldn't look away. She wanted what that couple had. That intimacy, that closeness. The clear passion between the two of them.

Heaven help her, Celeste had thought she'd given up on that longing three years ago. She realized she'd been fooling herself. She'd simply fallen for the wrong man.

She turned to see Reid watching the other couple also. His fist seemed to clench even tighter at his side.

"We should get cleaned up and dried off," he told her, gesturing to the building behind them that housed the shower and spa facilities.

But her feet wouldn't move. She didn't want this moment to end. The world around them seemed to fall away. Her vision zeroed in on one thing only—the man standing before her. The hunger in his eyes was as clear as the sunny sky above. Could he see that same hunger in her own?

"Lunch will be waiting for us soon," he reminded her. "We can use the time to go over your thoughts on ways to advertise this as part of the resort package."

It took a moment for her to register exactly what he was saying. How could she have forgotten even for a moment? She was only here because Reid was after her professional feedback.

While she stood here like a fool entertaining

all sorts of romantic fantasies, Reid was simply utilizing her for her marketing expertise. His only concern was for his business.

The realization was like more cold water splashing over her skin. How could she have not learned her lesson? Technically, she was nothing more than Reid's employee.

Celeste certainly cleaned up well.

Reid watched as she found him at the wooden table where they'd be eating an authentic Jamaican lunch. She wore leather sandals, lace-covered shorts that showed off her long shapely legs and a thin-strapped tank top. She hadn't bothered to dry her hair and wore it in a loose pile atop her head.

She was a breathtakingly stunning woman.

It wasn't easy, but Reid was trying hard to ignore the sudden awkwardness that had developed between them. He could pinpoint exactly when it had happened. That darned couple with the passionate kiss atop the waterfall. Usually, the PDA of other people didn't bother him or so much as give him pause. He worked at a tropical resort that hosted numbers of couples, after all. But watching that kiss made him realize how badly he wanted to kiss Celeste.

That was unacceptable.

She was essentially working for him. After

she left the resort, their paths may never cross again.

Oh, and there was also that whole other part where she'd been engaged to one of his closest friends. All that, on top of where he was in his life right now, Reid knew better than to acknowledge his growing attraction to a woman so clearly off-limits.

He cursed under his breath as she reached the table and sat down across from him. The smile she flashed him seemed forced and uncertain. She was aware of the awkwardness between them also.

Damn.

They still had a whole afternoon together. Not to mention all the activities scheduled for tomorrow. And the day after.

Maybe this whole thing hadn't been such a good idea. There was something developing between them that he hadn't expected or been prepared for.

Maybe he was deluding himself, but he was certain whatever was happening between them was mutual. That fact only made it all the worse.

He had a company to run, a devastated mother to look after, and he had to protect the family business from his reckless and disloyal father.

Nowhere in the scenario was there room to

pursue any kind of relationship, let alone with a woman who'd once been engaged to one of his best friends.

"You look none worse for the wear," he said in a rather lame attempt at conversation.

Lord, he could use some of the rum punch this place was known for. Unfortunately, the next leg of this particular package happened to involve driving an ATV.

The waitress appeared with two loaded plates and a couple bottles of water before Celeste had a chance to respond.

"Hope you like hot and spicy."

She shrugged. "Depends on the heat level. Too much makes me uncomfortable."

He really couldn't read anything into that statement. Though he was sorely tempted to ask her if they were still speaking about the jerk chicken.

"I'll have a write-up ready for you before the morning. I made sure to dictate some notes into my phone before showering just now," she said.

She had turned all business.

Probably for the best anyway. But he found he'd lost some of his appetite. For her part, Celeste was barely picking at her own plate.

Reid took another bite and relished the punishing heat of the scotch bonnet pepper on his tongue. The silence between them grew. Finally, he threw his napkin down on his plate. Shameful waste of authentic jerk chicken but he didn't want any more.

"Something the matter?" Celeste asked.

This was ridiculous. They were both mature adults. Maybe it was time to address the proverbial elephant in the room. Yet another one.

"Yeah, I happen to have something on my mind," he admitted.

She raised an eyebrow in question.

"About what happened back there," he continued. "After we were done climbing."

Her eyes grew wide.

"Maybe we should talk about it," he added.

"Maybe we should. What would you like to say?" Her question sounded like a dare.

Well, he could play the game as well anyone. "I think we got caught up in an exciting moment. What about you?"

Her lips tightened into a thin line before she answered him. "I see. That's the conclusion you came to then?"

He nodded. "I'm interested in your opinion, however."

A glimmer sparked in her eyes before she leaned in closer to him over the table. "By that you mean you'd like me to confirm your convenient take on the matter so that you can rest easy."

"What?"

"Don't worry, Reid. We can forget the moment even happened. And ignore everything else too, for that matter. We'll play our roles as contract employee and boss man. That's the way you want things, isn't it?"

"Yes!" he said without taking the time to think. "I mean, no," he then corrected after a beat. "I mean, I don't know."

They were starting to attract the attention of the other diners.

The waitress approached, a look of concern as she eyed their still-full plates. "Is the food not to your liking, sir? Madam?"

"It's very good," he answered, not taking his eyes off the woman who had him so vexed at the moment.

"It's delicious, thank you," Celeste answered, somehow summoning a smile.

He'd been wrong. This was not the time or place to try to have this conversation. What did she want him to say anyway? It wasn't as if he could admit there was some kind of attraction there.

What good would that do either of them?

"Unfortunately, we're short on time," he explained to the waitress who didn't look any less concerned after their exchange. "If we could settle the bill. We'll be sure to come back another time," he lied. The chances of him coming back here with Celeste seemed slim to none right about now.

In fact, he'd be lucky if she didn't ditch the whole idea of his proposal and leave him to his own devices. That thought settled like a brick of disappointment in his chest. And though he was loath to admit it, the feeling had nothing to do with his professional goals.

At least the next activity would be on dry land.

Celeste followed Reid through the tree line down the dirt path where they were to meet their ATV driving guide. At least out of the water she wouldn't be tempted to look at Reid's chiseled chest and tanned, muscular arms. And she wouldn't notice how strikingly dark his sandy blond hair turned when it was wet. Nor the way his tanned skin glistened when wet.

He'd almost kissed her.

But he'd made himself stop, as if he'd immediately regretted the near lapse. She didn't want to acknowledge just how much that wounded her. Or why.

For then she'd have to admit what a glutton for punishment she was. She'd gone down this route before. Men like Reid and Jack knew exactly how to shut down their attraction or even affection for a woman when they realized she wasn't good enough for them.

She'd let her guard down and fooled herself into thinking that Reid might be different from Jack. Would she ever learn?

Finally, they reached a convoy of parked all-terrain vehicles, some of them were caked over almost completely with mud. Clearly, she'd overdressed for the occasion. By contrast, Reid had changed into dark green camouflage canvas shorts and a black T-shirt. His attire seemed much more appropriate. Looked like she should have gone over the details more carefully.

A guide came out of one of the banana-leaf roofed huts and the two men shook hands. After another safety lecture and being fitted with helmets, they climbed into one of the vehicles.

"You sure you don't want to drive one yourself?" Reid asked her, though they'd gone over this on the charter boat this morning.

"I'm sure. I have no desire to race down muddy embankments and treacherous curves in an open-top vehicle barely larger than a golf cart." She knew she sounded overly critical but she wasn't in the best of moods currently. This definitely wasn't an activity she would choose for herself when picking out an itinerary. In fact, she wasn't sure how to write about it in a way that might make it sound enticing.

"Let's go then."

With that, Reid revved the engine and peeled out into the wooded terrain. Celeste gritted her teeth. She'd been on smoother roller coasters. Reid was pushing the vehicle to the top edge of the speedometer. Trees and bushes zipped past her line of vision, her whole body jostled and bounced in the seat. He was driving perilously close to the edge of the cliff and she had to focus on her breathing as if in meditation to avoid a full-fledged panic attack. She thought for sure he'd slow down as they approached a hairpin turn, but if anything, he seemed to accelerate. Celeste could have sworn they were riding on only the two side wheels for a brief moment.

Without warning, he suddenly veered into a more densely wooded area. Branches and brush whipped at the face mask of her helmet. Her panic grew by several notches.

The petrifying drive seemed to be having an opposite effect on Reid. Laughing and completely at ease, he was fully enjoying this. The next bump lifted her clear off the seat despite the tight seat belt. She landed back down with a thud that rattled her spine. Good thing she hadn't eaten much of the lunch earlier. No doubt it would have come up and lodged in her throat. Or worse.

An eternity seemed to go by before they

turned back onto the beaten path. Reid started to slow the car and eventually came to a blessed stop. Reid let out another excited whoop and put the car in gear at the end of the line of the others.

Celeste uttered a small prayer of thanks to whichever deity was listening then wasted no time removing her helmet and jumping out of the car. Running to the nearest tree, she braced herself against the trunk and sucked in some much-needed air.

It wasn't long before she heard his footsteps behind her. "Uh…are you all right?"

Celeste summoned all the effort she could in order to try to keep her voice steady. She failed. "Did you have to go quite so fast? And you left the path. In fact, you ignored it altogether!" she blurted out, all too aware of the accusatory tone of her voice.

"Going fast is sort of the point," he countered. "And the guide said the path was a recommendation only. That more experienced drivers could use their best judgment."

"You consider yourself experienced, then, do you?" She hated the high pitch of her voice. But, rational or not, she'd really been scared back there.

A muscle twitched in his jaw. "I do, as a matter of fact. I grew up riding such vehicles. As well as snowmobiles."

Of course he had. Was there nothing he wasn't good at? Or didn't have experience with? Whereas this was the first time she'd so much as sat on an ATV. The closest she'd come was the subway. Yet another example of how different they were, how their worlds had nothing in common. History repeating itself.

"Well, did you think about what might have happened if you'd lost control, even for a split second? I have a mother, a sister and a niece who need me alive to provide for them!" she almost shouted, then forced herself to calm down and take a breath. "I just need a minute to regain some balance here," she told him unevenly.

Reid took a step closer to her and frowned. "Take your time. You do look a little pale."

"I'll be fine." Once her pulse finally settled. Only that didn't seem like it was going to be anytime soon.

Just breathe.

"Why didn't you say anything?" he wanted to know.

Celeste didn't bother to answer. The fact was, she'd wanted to. But she hated that she'd gotten so panicky, that she'd felt so weak. She hated the idea of having to admit it to him. She'd just prayed that he'd eventually slow the cursed vehicle down. Only he hadn't.

As if reading her thoughts, Reid continued,

"Look, I'm sorry if you were nervous or scared during the ride. And I'm even more sorry that I didn't notice. But I assure you that you were never in any danger. I knew exactly what I was doing."

That made one of them, Celeste thought.

CHAPTER SEVEN

THE FOLLOWING MORNING Celeste decided she was going to do absolutely nothing that day. Reid didn't have anything booked for them until tomorrow. Thank heavens for that small mercy. She punched her fluffy pillow and turned over in bed to stare at the ceiling.

So why did she miss seeing him so much already? Why had last night seemed so empty and boring? Barely twelve hours had passed since she'd seen him last and it wasn't as if they'd parted on the most positive note. Even after the awkward boat ride back to the resort where neither one had so much as spoken a word to the other, she wondered if that strained silence would have been preferable to the solitary dinner she'd had on her balcony before retiring early.

She'd somehow grown used to his company. That did not bode well at all.

Her phone screen lit up with a text on the bedside table next to her. She didn't need to look to know that it was Tara. She and her mother had been trying to get a hold of her all day yesterday. Celeste had no intention of returning the call just yet. Whatever it was could wait. She needed some downtime to process everything that had happened in the last twenty-four hours. The last thing that would allow her to do that would be to have any kind of toxic conversation with her family. If it was a true emergency, she knew they'd move all manner of heaven and earth to contact her.

No. Today she was going to linger in bed, then quietly meditate. Maybe afterward she'd take one of the yoga classes offered at the resort gym. Then she may or may not spend the afternoon in a lounge chair by the pool. Or back in her room with the gripping book she'd been neglecting.

Her idea of utopia. Usually, anyway.

Though she'd be alone the whole time. Normally, that would not have given her pause. In fact, it was the way she preferred to spend time on vacation.

She uttered a curse under her breath. The only reason she was questioning that now was because of one sandy blond masculine CEO with eyes the color of the deep ocean at sunrise and a dark beard. Celeste had never even liked facial hair before this. But on Reid, all she could think about was running her fingers through it. Or how it might feel against her skin.

She bolted upright before that thread of thought could go any further. Maybe her wayward thoughts about him were simply a result of her self-imposed celibacy these past few years. Maybe she'd do well to find a random single man on the beach and invite him back to her room for a no-strings-attached fun-filled afternoon.

Tara would be delighted for her.

Ha! As if she'd manage to let go of her inhibitions to ever allow that. As if she'd ever be so carefree. No. That was more her sister's style. That would take a level of lightheartedness Celeste had never achieved in her life. Plus, she didn't think it would do any good toward ridding her brain of Reid Evanson imaginings.

The ring of her room landline jarred her out of her musings. Now she was concerned. Maybe there was some kind of emergency back home if her mother and Tara were trying to reach her through the hotel phone service. She grabbed the receiver.

"Hello?"

"Ms. Frajedi. Good morning. This is Prita at the front desk."

"Is everything all right?"

"Absolutely," Prita answered cheerfully with the slightest creole accent.

A wave of relief washed over her at the announcement.

"I'm just calling to let you know that you have a spa package waiting for you. You can come in anytime today."

"The spa? I didn't book anything at the spa."

"This is complimentary, Ms. Frajedi."

"I don't understand."

"It was booked at the direction of Mr. Evanson."

"I see."

"The package includes a full massage, facial, followed by a manicure and pedicure. It will take a few hours if you'd like to decide on a time."

"Thank you, Prita. I'd like to think about it and get back to you."

"Certainly, Ms. Frajedi. I'll give you the line to the spa and you can contact them directly."

Celeste made note of the number and disconnected the call. Reid had set her up with a day of luxurious pampering. She'd be a fool to turn it down.

Why had he done it?

Was this some manner of apology for the way things had turned out yesterday? Or was she to approach it as his employee and give him feedback on her spa experience? Perhaps he'd simply wanted to do something nice for her?

The latter was the least likely possibility.

So many lines were blurred between them now. They were former enemies but now she was technically working for him. She'd been engaged to one of his good friends.

She couldn't get the thought of kissing him out of her head. Or the way his touch had warmed her skin every time he'd caught her while climbing the falls. How it had felt to be embraced in his arms when he'd congratulated her afterward.

Enough already! What a pointless waste of brain cells to go over all of it repeatedly in her head. What was the use?

So much for staying in bed all day. Suddenly, she was too restless and wired up to just lay there. A day at the spa wasn't such a bad idea.

With a deep sigh, Celeste got up and made her way to the shower. She had some pampering to prepare herself for.

Thanks to Reid.

Reid's focus was completely shot. For what had to be the umpteenth time during their morning meeting, he tried to lure his concentration back to what Alex was saying. Instead, his mind kept wandering to thinking about what Celeste might be doing at this very moment. Had she taken him up yet on the spa offer? Was she there even now, lying on a massage table having some of the tension kneaded out of her muscles?

Would she accept his overture as the apology that it was intended to be?

Alex was making another point. "And I've spoken with the entertainment committee to put together a showing of *The Nutcracker* ballet with you dancing the major roles."

Reid nodded. "That's good, thank—"

Wait a minute.

Reid dropped his pen on the desk. "Ha-ha. That's really funny, partner."

"Just checking to see if you were paying attention. Where is your head at this morning, man?"

If he only knew. "I have a lot on my mind."

"Including the woman who's been helping you pull together a potential marketing campaign?"

Reid quirked his eyebrow. "Why do you ask that?"

"Let's just say you haven't quite been the same since she arrived on the island."

So it was that obvious.

Luckily, his partner wasn't the type to delve into his personal life. Not usually, anyway.

"How's that whole project going anyway?" Alex asked, reverting back to business matters.

Reid wasn't quite sure how to answer. Where exactly did things stand now between Celeste and himself? "We just started yesterday."

Alex tilted his head. "And?"

"And we have a couple more excursions on the schedule tomorrow. She'll provide a written analysis and suggestions for each one we take."

Though, after the way yesterday had turned out, Reid wasn't even sure if Celeste was even still on board with it. He was half-afraid she'd already made the decision to end their agreement. Something told him she wouldn't do that. That she took her professional commitments far too seriously.

In fact, he was banking on it.

Still, she hadn't called to thank him or so much as acknowledge the spa day he'd arranged for her. An image of her lying on a massage table with only a narrow towel draped around her luscious curves flashed in his mind.

His partner was staring at him expectantly. Oh, yeah. He'd asked him a question, hadn't he?

Something about what he and Celeste were working on together. Reid decided to stick the truth. For the most part, anyway.

"Things are complicated between Celeste

and me," he admitted, rubbing his forehead. "There's a bit of a history."

"I see," Alex responded. "And is that the only complication?"

"Absolutely," Reid lied. It wasn't an egregiously big lie however. Because he'd made something of a decision last night. As he'd lain there thinking about Celeste and the way she'd felt in his arms, he'd come to the conclusion that his dealings with her had to change.

From this point forward, he would maintain a safer distance. He would be at his utmost professional as they worked together. Though not technically his direct employee, Celeste was indeed doing work for him. He would treat her like the contractor that she was. No more touching, no more teasing. And definitely no more imagining her naked on a massage table or in the shower.

"Good," Alex interrupted that risky train of thought. "I'm interested to see what the two of you come up with. What's next?"

If Celeste didn't withdraw from the project altogether, they were due for a rather sublime activity tomorrow. "We're scheduled to visit the flower garden in St. Anne's Parish." An activity that would require no physical contact whatsoever, Reid thought with no small amount of gratefulness. The family owned and run botanical garden attracted tourists from all over the world to admire the striking flora that graced so much of the island. After a tour of the flower beds and exotic plants and trees, the excursion included some light shopping and a home-cooked meal.

Surely, he could get through something like that without laying his hands on Celeste's tempting body?

Piece of cake.

To make matters even better, they'd be fully clothed. No swimsuits involved for this outing. He wouldn't have to force his gaze away from the tiny dimple in Celeste's luscious thigh. Or the way her suit fit her like a glove and accentuated all those glorious curves.

"You just drifted off again, my friend."

Reid uttered a small curse. Thank heavens Alex had no idea exactly where his mind had drifted off to.

Who was he kidding? Celeste wasn't even here and he couldn't get her out of his head. He had his work cut out for him if he was going to maintain a professional distance tomorrow.

"Sorry. I was just mentally going over my to-do list." Another fib. He hadn't been this slippery with his friend and partner at any other time before this. He was behaving uncharacteristically in so many ways, he'd lost count.

Alex suddenly stood, apparently giving up on any kind of productive meeting given the state of Reid's mental sharpness at the moment.

"I should go get started on mine," he said, then turned to leave. He stopped at the door and turned back with a playful smile. "You sure you won't reconsider the *Nutcracker* gig now?"

"I'm sure, my man. No one needs to see me in tights."

Alex released a bark of laughter before exiting.

Reid turned to stare out at the glass wall behind his desk. In the distance, the ocean sparkled like a sea of precious gems. The sun shone bright in a clear, azure-blue sky. Another beautiful day in paradise.

The building that housed the spa could be seen at the edge of the property. Was she there now?

Reid stood and closed the lid of his laptop. Nothing wrong with taking a walk in that direction. He hadn't even been outside yet today. Some fresh Caribbean air would do him some good right now. He definitely wasn't trying to seek Celeste out. And if he did run into her merely by chance, what would be wrong with that?

No harm, no foul, he reassured himself. He'd

simply be checking on a contract employee. Fifteen minutes later, after catching no sign of her, Reid resigned himself to acknowledging that their paths would not be crossing this morning. He also had to acknowledge the disappointment he felt.

CHAPTER EIGHT

Right on time.

Celeste's cell phone screen lit up with a text message as she was walking down the concrete pathway to the entrance of the resort property.

I'm here a couple minutes early. See you soon. R

She'd be arriving right at the time they'd agreed to meet at the bellhop desk to board the shuttle bus that would take them to the Flower Forest. Looked like Reid didn't want to take any chances that she'd be late. Or that she wouldn't show. If she was being fair, she would admit he couldn't be blamed for being uncertain. She hadn't so much as dropped him a thank-you text for the extravagant day of decadence he'd treated her to yesterday.

Even worse, she'd seen him approaching the spa building as she was leaving but had ducked for cover and turned the other way. Not that she'd meant to avoid him. But she had just needed one full day away from him to regain her equilibrium.

Truth be told, she was also a little embarrassed. Her reaction to the ATV ride weighed on her. Reid probably saw her as weak and fearful of new activities. It galled her to appear that way to anyone, let alone a man like him. The temperature dropped several degrees as she entered the air-conditioned concierge lobby. She spotted Reid right away, but then he was particularly hard to miss. A head taller than most of the people in the room, he was dressed in khaki shorts and another formfitting T-shirt, blue this time. She had no doubt the rich color would serve to heighten the golden hue of his eyes.

Her conclusion was confirmed when she reached him. Yep, a girl could get lost in those beautiful golden depths if she didn't check herself.

Celeste would have to make sure to check herself.

"You made it."

She wasn't imagining the relief in his voice. He'd been afraid she wasn't going to show.

"All refreshed and ready to go," she answered with a smile. "Thank you for my day of pampering yesterday. I feel like a new woman."

His responding smile sent a bolt of awareness through her core.

"I'm glad you enjoyed it."

"Shall we?" Celeste prompted, before another one of those awkward silences could ensue that seemed to be so very frequent between them.

Reid nodded and led her outside to the waiting town car and held the back door open for her before climbing in the other side. Within moments they were pulling out of the long stone driveway and onto the main road. It always took Celeste a moment to adjust to the sensation of being driven on the opposite side of the street than what she was used to in the States.

Reid flipped open a console between their feet to reveal an assortment of drinks and snacks. "Can I get you anything?"

Celeste accepted some water and a rich chocolate bar that seemed to melt in her mouth when she bit into it. Between hours at the spa yesterday and this luxurious ride, she could get used to this lifestyle. City life was overrated.

"So, tell me about this flower garden," she said between bites.

Reid uncapped a bottle of iced tea as he answered. "It's called the Flower Forest. It's one of the first excursions we contracted out after acquiring the resort. Owned and operated by the same family for generations. Now it's just the matriarch and her son and daughter. All three are delightful people. A bit on the traditional side. You'll enjoy meeting them."

"I look forward to it." She realized she was looking forward to the whole day, in fact. Unlike the adventurous feats of the previous excursions, this one sounded low-key and relaxing.

She'd have a chance to spend some time with Reid without a constant stream of adrenaline clouding her judgment. Maybe they'd even enjoy each other's company.

No. That was hardly the goal for today. She had to keep that fact in mind. They weren't a couple out enjoying an island getaway. They were barely friends, if one were to be completely accurate. Boundaries were important here.

Half an hour later, they pulled onto a gravel road and eventually came to a thick, green tree line.

Celeste had to suck in a breath when she exited the car at the sheer amount of color that greeted her. A flowing river could be heard behind the trees. The fragrant scent of exotic flowers filled the air. The entire scene could have been painted by a talented landscape artist.

Oh, yeah. This was much more up her alley than a jostling ride in an open-air vehicle as it straddled a cliff edge.

"Oh! It's so beautiful, Reid. Just lovely." This would be the easiest write-up she'd ever done.

A rotund woman who appeared to be in her early sixties appeared from behind a wooden gate and approached them. She was trailed by a young man and woman. Each had the same facial structure and eye shape. It was clear they were siblings.

"Mr. Reid. So nice to see you again," the woman said, giving Reid a hug and a small peck on the cheek.

"Uma, the pleasure's all mine," Reid answered over her head.

"You remember my son and daughter, Rinna and Theo," Uma added. The siblings nodded in acknowledgment.

"Of course." Reid motioned to where Celeste stood behind them.

"And I'd like you all to meet Celeste. She's a colleague of mine. She's going to help us bring some more attention and visitors to this lovely slice of paradise you have here."

Celeste reached out her hand but Uma ignored it and hugged her instead, as well. She mustered a smile as she returned the older woman's embrace but it was forced.

The word *colleague* had never sounded so disappointing.

"I have a confession to make," Reid said in a low voice as they trailed behind Rinna and Theo, their tour guides. Uma had left for the kitchen to start preparing the meal.

"What's that?" Celeste asked, her curiosity peaked. What in the world could he be referring to?

"I was a little concerned you'd back out of coming along today. After you know…the last time."

So he had been worried. Celeste felt a pang of regret. She had a stellar reputation as a competent and efficient businesswoman. To think that she'd given Reid the impression of unreliability would weigh heavily on her for some time to come.

Her professional reputation was a matter she took very seriously and an accomplishment she had worked very hard for over the years. Just made for another reason why she had to suppress whatever this attraction was between her and Reid. She had too much at stake. Theo stopped in front of a tree and turned to face them.

"This is Frangipani," Theo explained, pointing to the small tree adorned with white flowers. Celeste could smell the rich perfume of the petals where she stood.

They moved on. Theo and Rinna took turns pointing out and naming various flowers, bushes, and trees. Celeste was fascinated by the hibiscus flowers, which she'd seen on countless tea bag label ingredients but now had a picture of what the plant looked like.

All in all, it was a fascinating stroll. The weather was perfect, warm yet not muggy. A gentle breeze fanned her skin. By the time their tour ended, she felt both entertained and educated. A perfect tagline to advertise the attraction.

They'd reached the banks of the river when Uma came out to summon them to lunch. In moments, they were seated at a wooden picnic table by the water enjoying a mouthwatering meal of fried fish, rice and plantain.

"You were right," Celeste remarked between bites. "They are a delightful family. And Uma's a wonderful cook."

"Do you think you have a good idea of how to frame the description of this place?"

There it was again. Reid's sole focus was on the mission at hand. She wanted to kick herself for feeling any disappointment at his remark. It wasn't Reid's fault that she kept forgetting the true objective here. If anything, she should be thanking him for leading her back on track.

She nodded in response to his question. "I think so. The delicious food will play a major role."

Reid put his fork down and leaned toward her over the table. "Tell me something."

"Yes?" Celeste was fully expecting a question about her thoughts on the Flower Forest and what sort of features she would highlight in any summary she put together for him. So, his next words threw her completely off guard.

"Have you moved on? From your engagement to Jack and how it ended?"

Whoa. She had definitely not seen that coming.

Reid had an almost uncanny knack for throwing her off her feet. She swallowed the last bite she'd taken quickly, before she risked having it lodged in her throat.

She wasn't sure how to answer his question. If Reid was asking her if she'd met someone else in the past three years, the answer was no. But in every other sense, she'd moved on.

He suddenly looked away, out toward the water. "I'm sorry. I shouldn't have asked you that. It's none of my business."

"But you did ask. Why?"

"I'm not sure." He gave her a tight smile. "Like I said. I shouldn't have. I have no excuse for asking it."

Theo approached them before she could respond. He carried a sleek-looking professional camera. "Reid. Celeste. I hoped I might be able to take a few photos of the two of you."

Celeste couldn't decide if she was relieved or

annoyed at the interruption. A little bit of both probably, she'd have to admit.

"I'm trying to do my own little bit of publicity for Mom. Just some photos to add to our website."

Reid looked at her in question. "That okay with you?"

Celeste shrugged. "Sure. Why not?"

They turned and smiled for Theo who snapped several shots in rapid succession.

"Let's do some by the water, yeah?" Theo suggested, and led them to the riverbank. "And I hate to ask…"

Reid gave him an indulgent smile. "Anything for you, Theo. What is it?"

"It's just that we're trying to appeal to a wider audience. Mainly couples. We seem to only get families with children. I was thinking it couldn't hurt to emphasize the romantic aspects of this place." He gestured around him.

Uh-oh. Celeste could guess where Theo was headed. He confirmed her suspicions. "You two mind posing like you're a real couple? You know, just so the photos look authentic?"

Neither one of them could seem to come up with an answer. Theo must have sensed their mutual discomfort. "Uh… Never mind. Forget I asked."

A pang of guilt settled in Celeste's stomach.

What was the harm in a couple of photos? Theo, his mom and his sister had been the most perfect of hosts; gracious and accommodating. The least she and Reid could do was playact for a couple of stills.

"I'm okay with it if you are," she uttered, not quite able to look Reid in the eyes as she spoke.

Reid gave a slight shrug. "Sure. Go for it, Theo."

Theo flashed them a wide smile. "Thanks! So, just step together closer and, Reid, put your arm around Celeste's shoulders."

Reid did as instructed and Theo snapped away.

"That's great, you two. You both are naturals at this." He looked at the camera screen with a pleased smile. "It looks real. Like you guys are really together."

Celeste had to suppress an internal groan. Then things went from bad to worse.

"How about a pretend kiss?" Theo suggested.

CHAPTER NINE

REID HAD EVERY intention of simply dropping the slightest peck on Celeste's cheek. At the most, he might have softly brushed his lips along the corner of her mouth.

But somehow, after Theo made his suggestion, Reid's lips found hers and he seemed to have lost control of his intentions.

She tasted of berries and chocolate, her lips soft and luscious under his. Someone sighed heavily. He couldn't even tell which one of them it was. Her arms went up around his neck and it was all the invite he needed to pull her closer, deepen the kiss. Time seemed to stand still, their audience forgotten. Nothing of the outside mattered for him now. His one and only focus was the woman in his arms and how it felt to hold her, to kiss her.

He'd been imagining this, he had to admit. He'd had dreams at night where he held her, touched her, took her mouth with his exactly as he was doing now. The reality of it was so much more than he could have guessed. The clicking of Theo's camera suddenly registered in his brain. He couldn't be sure which one of them broke the contact first. Only that he felt the loss like a physical pang as Celeste pulled back and looked up at him. Her cheeks were flushed, her lips reddened from his mouth. It excited him to think that he'd been the one to put that color into her face, and her reaction to him only served to heighten his own desire.

"Reid?" she whispered softly, low enough so that he was sure Theo couldn't hear her question over the noise of his picture taking.

He wanted desperately to answer her. Not verbally but by kissing her again, he wanted to show her how much he desired her, how much of an effect she was having on him.

Theo's voice charged through his desire-fogged mind. "That's perfect, you two. These will work great. Let's move onto a different location, yeah?"

Reid couldn't seem to make his limbs work. He knew he should let her go. He knew they should turn around and follow Theo who had already stepped away and was walking toward the garden. But he couldn't so much as tear his gaze from Celeste's face.

Her breath had gone shallow. The one word

question she'd uttered as simply his name still hung heavily in the air.

He couldn't help it, he touched his finger to her bottom lip and trailed it lower to her jaw.

Confusion grew in her eyes. "Uh. Theo's left. You don't have to keep pretending now."

The words felt like ice water thrown at him. They served just as effectively to pull him out of his desire-filled daze.

How foolish of him. Looked like only one of them had simply been pretending.

She'd never been good at pretending. The lines always became blurry for her. They certainly had just now. How much of Reid's kiss was real? How much was fake?

Dear heavens. She had to admit that everything she'd felt as soon as his lips touched hers felt one hundred percent real. Well, she'd do well to snap out of it. Reid had already moved forward. He turned to see if she was following him.

"Coming?" he asked, completely nonchalant. Unlike her, he seemed far from affected in any way by the kiss they'd shared.

The fake kiss.

Celeste forced her feet to move and reached his side. Together they walked over to where Theo stood waiting for them by the Frangipani tree he'd told them about earlier when they'd first arrived. He motioned for them to go stand in front of it.

"How about you two hold hands?" Theo suggested after they'd complied with his request. Reid reached for her and she swore a bolt of electricity shot through her arm as she took his hand.

She had to clamp down on all this emotion. She couldn't let herself continue this way. She was only here in Jamaica for a few more short days. Soon, this whole adventure of a vacation would be over. She'd go back to her old life, her demanding job, and her draining family. She had neither the time nor the energy to spend her days pining over a man from her past. A man who was tied to her one majorly disastrous failed relationship. That life was her reality, those were the things waiting for her back home. A life full of responsibility and consequences. This was all a fantasy, a fake portrait that was meant to go into brochures and on websites.

It wouldn't do for her to forget that for even the slightest moment.

"You're not really smiling," Reid informed her through the side of his mouth. By contrast, he looked like a man thoroughly enjoying the day.

"Sorry. I'm not really good at this acting

thing." Celeste forced her mouth to curve into a smile.

"Really? You could have fooled me."

What was that supposed to mean? She probably didn't even want to know.

"Let's just get this over with," Reid added. His grip against her palm lightened ever so slightly.

Well, that comment certainly cemented it. If she'd harbored any illusions that Reid was in any way as moved by their kiss earlier as she was, she could rest assured that he wasn't.

If only she could be like the tree behind her, Celeste thought, feigning another smile for Theo's camera. If only she could completely shed her unwanted feelings like they were discarded leaves. And then start anew. A whole new beginning, completely leaving the past behind.

The first metaphorical leaf she would drop would be her fraught and complicated feelings toward the man currently holding her hand.

Rinna approached them as they wrapped up the last few photos. It had taken some effort but somehow Celeste had willed her breath to return to a normal pace.

Well, as normal as she'd ever experienced while in Reid's presence.

"Momma asks that you two stay for dinner," the young woman announced when she reached them. "She says there's some type of holiday parade blocking the roads near the city. So you may as well wait it out."

As if on cue, Reid's phone lit up and he blew out a frustrated sigh when he glanced at it. "My driver has just confirmed exactly that." He turned to her. "Looks like we'll be here a bit longer than intended. Did you have any plans?"

Celeste shook her head. Of course, she didn't. She was here solo, after all. A warring flurry of uncertainty tightened her chest. Part of her didn't want this day to end. Another more sensible part warned her that any prolonging of time spent with Reid was a lethal threat to her inner peace.

"Excellent." Rinna clapped her hands in front of her chest. "I'll go let Momma know. She loves having company. We'll eat in about half an hour."

"This is good," Theo added after his sister left. "This will give you two a chance to see the holiday lights we set up this year. We decorated many of the trees. It's beautiful after dark."

"I'm looking forward to it," Celeste answered. She'd always been a sucker for Christmas trees and the sparkling lights during the season. One of the few aspects of the holidays she hadn't grown to resent.

Theo lifted his camera. "I'm going to go upload these images. You two take your time. See you at the house in a bit."

"Sorry about this," Reid said after the other man had left. "Things work differently on the islands. Holiday parades sometimes pop up without advance warning."

"It's all right, Reid," she answered. "Like I said, I didn't have any plans." She wondered if he thought that was pathetic.

"Well, good. If you'll excuse me, I should make a few phone calls given the change in my return time. I'm afraid I was due to meet someone who'll be arriving on the island tonight. Alex will have to take over."

Of course, unlike her, Reid would have a full schedule. No doubt this delay caused all sorts of disruption for him. A business owner like him had all sorts of demands on his time.

She wondered if one of the phone calls he was making was a personal one. Did it have anything to do with whoever he was expecting to fly in? He'd never mentioned being involved with a woman but why would he? It wasn't like it was any of her business. And though Celeste had never actually seen him with a lady so far on this trip, that meant nothing. She'd only been on the island a few days. While she'd spent a considerable amount of time during those days fantasizing and thinking about him, she'd steadfastly avoided wondering about his social life.

Now that she'd been confronted with the possibility he was attached, she felt even more foolish for pining for him for even a moment. Seemed she was a magnet for rejection. To imagine that someone like Reid would ever see her as anything like a romantic girlfriend was downright folly. She'd fallen for that fantasy once before, only to have reality come straight back and slap her into the truth. Men like Reid didn't end up with women like her.

No doubt the mysterious arrival was a beautiful, successful, and accomplished gem of a woman. Perhaps she was the model from the magazine cover she'd seen at the airport. Or maybe an actress. She vaguely recalled seeing a different photo several months back of Reid at some movie awards ceremony, attending as the guest of a Hollywood starlet.

She glanced at Reid's back now as he spoke into his cell phone, braced against one of the trees a few feet away. Slowly, she made her way toward the river. Watching the water stream by might be a soothing way to iron out her frazzled nerves. The whole day had been an emotional roller coaster. Correction, her whole trip had been a harrowing series of ups and downs. Definitely not what she'd expected to be in store for her. Just one more curve thrown at her. To think, she'd been so excited to leave the city behind her for several days.

Maybe this should have been the one year she stayed home for the holidays. The sadness the season always invoked in her might have actually been preferable to the assault to her peace that had been this trip so far.

She heard his footsteps behind her and instinctively took another step forward in a futile attempt at creating some distance between them. She really could use some time to think alone.

"Careful," Reid's voice warned from behind her. "You're awfully close to the edge there. The ground can be slippery. Unless you're looking for an impromptu swim."

An illogical surge of annoyance speared through her. She was a grown woman. One who certainly didn't need to be told what to do. In sheer defiance born of rebellion, she took another step.

Only to prove the worth of Reid's word of warning. Her foot slid out from underneath her as it landed on a slick patch of mud. She felt the shocking splash of water an instant later. Reid's shouted curse was immediately followed by another splash as he jumped in after her. Why in the world would he do that? She could swim, for heaven's sake. Now they'd both be a soaked, river-slimed mess. She opened her lips to tell him so only to have her mouth flooded with said slimy water. That couldn't be good.

"Hang on," Reid shouted over the splash of the water.

Even in the shock of her fall, only one thought crammed through her mind.

She hated that he'd been right. And that he was now attempting to rescue her.

Reid bit out another curse as he landed in the steadily flowing river. Grabbing Celeste by the waist, he began to hoist her onto the edge of the riverbank. Was she actually resisting? What the…?

He lifted her out of the water and followed her onto the land. "Are you all right? You didn't hurt yourself, did you?"

She ignored his question, posing one of her own. "Why did you do that?" she demanded to know crossly. "You did not need to jump in after me."

Well, if that didn't take the cake. "You have a funny way of saying thank you." Swiping the moisture off his face, he then ran his fingers through his hair.

Celeste was shooting fire at him. For helping her out of the water she'd fallen into, despite him having warned her.

He would never understand this woman, probably shouldn't even try. So he wanted to kick himself for the direction his next thoughts took him in. No woman should look that enticing dripping wet after a drenching in a green tinged, mossy body of water.

For that's exactly what she was. Enticing.

Her hair had turned a shade darker after the drenching, accenting the golden hue of her tanned skin. Her soaked white lace dress clung to her like a caress in all the right places. He had a clear view of her undergarments through the wet fabric of her clothes. Reid made himself avert his gaze. It wasn't easy.

He longed to slowly strip her of the dress, then rub his hands over every inch of her soaked skin to warm it up. His breath caught in his throat at the image. He couldn't deny it any longer. He wanted her. And he wanted her so badly it made him ache inside. How or when it had happened, he couldn't even try to place. Maybe it had all started that first day he'd seen her sprawled on a lounger on the beach. Perhaps it went back even further than that.

Not something he really wanted to examine

at the moment. The better question was what he was going to do about it.

"Honestly, Reid," she huffed as she stepped around him. "Now we're both a mess."

He blinked. "Are you actually upset that I helped you out of the water?"

"I didn't need rescuing," she declared and tried to push past him.

Without thinking, he reached out to take her by the elbow and turned her around to face him. "What is your deal?"

Her chin lifted in defiance. "I thought I already explained. I didn't need you to jump in after me. I'm perfectly capable of swimming out of a body of water."

He gave his head a shake. "Have you always been this difficult? I can't seem to remember."

It was the wrong thing to say. Celeste's eyes darkened with anger. "Is that what Jack told you?" she demanded to know. "That I'm difficult? That I'm hardly worth the effort? Did you two have fun talking about me and how sad and downright pathetic I looked waiting for him at the altar? Do you two get together at the bar on weekends and make fun of how ridiculous I looked on what should have been the happiest day of my life?"

Reid felt his jaw drop. Such an accusation

was the last thing he'd been expecting. "What? Of course not."

"What exactly are you denying, Reid? That you think I'm difficult? Or that I'm a pathetic, dejected discard? Or that you and Jack get a kick out of recalling my humiliation?"

He couldn't seem to find the words to respond. The things she was saying were downright preposterous. Little did she know, he thought Jack's behavior was inexcusable that day. Friend or not, it had been a cowardly and treacherous way to treat a woman. Let alone someone like Celeste.

She pulled her arm free from his grasp. "Never mind. I'm going to ask for a towel."

With that she trudged away toward the house. He caught up to her in mere strides, though he didn't dare reach for her again. For he was far too tempted to shake some sense into her. Then he would tell her how ridiculous a notion it was to hint that she'd been at all responsible for the way Jack had treated her. That she was far too good for him and always had been. And then he would quiet any further protest by crushing his lips to hers and tasting her again the way he wanted to so badly.

"For the record," he bit out. "Jack and I never discussed you after that day. Not once. Even when the subject of his averted wedding came up. The conversation never turned to talk about you specifically." Mainly because Reid wouldn't allow it, he added silently. "And we certainly don't laugh at you over beers at the local pub!"

"Yeah, right," she answered, not breaking her stride. He had several inches on her and much longer legs, but somehow it was an effort to keep pace with her. Her anger seemed to be propelling her forward. Or her desire to get away from him.

"What reason would I have to lie about that?"

She shrugged, still moving ahead. "I don't know. Some misplaced sense of loyalty your friend perhaps? I know how charming and convincing Jack can be."

Reid rubbed a frustrated hand down his face. "Why are we arguing about this? Now of all times?" But the answer occurred to him before he got the last word out.

She was thinking of Jack. She wanted to know if he asked about her, talked about her. And apparently, the answer mattered to her. Why else would she be so upset?

One thing was certain. The reverse was absolutely true. Even if Jack didn't think of her, Celeste still thought about her former fiancé. Jack was on her mind even at this very moment. Even after she'd spent the morning with Reid.

After he'd kissed her under the native tree, held her hand and smiled with her at Theo and his camera.

A fireball of anger seemed to ignite in his gut. His vision turned gray and he had to bite back a curse. He stopped in his tracks and let her continue forward. He would have to meet her at the house later. Right now he needed to be alone. He needed to try to think straight.

A task he couldn't seem to do well whenever Celeste was near.

"Oh, my!" Rinna cried out when she saw the state Celeste was in. "I see you fell into the water."

"We both did," Celeste announced and climbed up the porch steps. "Well, to be more accurate, I fell in. Then Reid jumped in after me. For some inexplicable reason."

"I see," Rinna said simply. She glanced in the distance behind where Celeste stood. "Where is Reid?"

Celeste was vaguely aware that he'd stopped following her at some point. Thank heavens he had. Or she might have turned to him then and there and asked him exactly what he thought of her. How he *felt* about her. She might have run the risk of having him come and say straight out what she suspected—that he liked her enough as a person. But that there could never be anything between them. Hence, she'd be making a fool of herself over a man yet again.

"Um...could I borrow a towel?" Celeste asked just Uma stepped out onto the porch from behind the screen door.

The older woman clapped a hand to her face. "Of course, dear. Come in and let's get you dry."

Celeste went up the stairs gratefully and went to step inside, only to have her ankle give out.

Uma and Rinna both jointly caught her just before she could hit the ground. "Are you all right, dear? Did you hurt yourself in the river?"

Celeste gave her head a shake. "I didn't think so. But I must have sprained it somehow during the fall. And then the walk to the house must have aggravated it." She rubbed a hand down her foot, which was starting to swell and bruise right before her eyes.

"Let's get you to the couch," Rinna suggested. "Theo's gone back out for more pictures. Can you try to stand without putting any weight on that foot?"

She didn't get a chance to answer. A deep masculine voice sounded from behind the three of them.

"I've got her."

A set of strong, muscular arms suddenly wrapped around her waist and under her bottom. The next instant she felt herself lifted into Reid's masculine embrace. Heaven help her, she took a moment to simply inhale the scent of him. The same mixture of citrus and sandalwood combined with mint, somehow still present despite the river water soaking his skin. Without giving herself a chance to think, she rested her forehead against his broad chest, taking comfort in the warmth of his skin against her cheek. Reid nuzzled his jaw against the top of her head. She didn't dare try to read anything into his action. He probably just felt bad for her.

"Does it hurt badly?" he asked, his voice smooth above her head.

"No. Not really. Just a little achy."

"Sorry about all this," he spoke low into her ear as he carried her farther inside and toward the couch.

Great. Now he was trying to take responsibility for her fall. "I'm not sure why you're apologizing."

"You're only here in the first place because of me."

"That may be. But I fell into the water on my own. Due to my own carelessness."

He exhaled deeply as he set her down on the couch. "Anyone ever tell you that you can be stubborn?" he asked.

Was it her imagination or did his hands linger around her body just a bit longer than was necessary after he set her down on the cushions? She looked up to find the smallest hint of a smile on his face.

"As a matter of fact, I do hear that from time to time."

The smile grew. "I'll bet."

A strange sensation tugged at her heart. The warmth of his touch still lingered over her wet skin. The man did something to her insides she couldn't recall feeling with anyone else ever. Not even the man she'd been prepared to marry.

Rinna appeared from behind them with a couple of pillows. She placed one behind her back and the other under the offending foot. Reid leaned over her. "May I?" he asked, gesturing to her leg.

She reluctantly agreed and he ran a gentle finger along the arch of her foot and around her ankle. Then he went up higher, toward her knee. Totally innocuous as it was, tingles of awareness rippled up her skin at his touch. Full-out kisses by other men had elicited less of a reaction from her than Reid simply examining her sore ankle. She had to suppress a shudder of reaction.

"It doesn't appear to be broken," he announced. "Just a sprain."

"You think so?"

"I'd place a wager on it if I had to." He nodded and gave her a teasing wink. "I've broken enough bones in my lifetime to be able to speak with some authority on the subject."

Celeste thanked the other woman for the pillows and allowed herself a groan of frustration. What a burden she was being to these people. And Reid, for that matter. All because she had been a careless klutz. She had no one else to blame but herself. Truth be told, she'd been distracted and dazed since that first day when she'd gone to find Santa only to discover Reid Evanson in his stead.

"Do you have any ice?" Reid asked Rinna.

"We do. But we can do even better than that. Momma has gone out to gather the plants she needs to mix up a medicinal balm." She laughed and shook her head. "I've had it applied to my various scrapes and bruises countless times over the years. She'll be back to prepare it soon. You'll start healing in no time," she reassured.

Celeste resisted the urge to ask if Uma might be able to come up with a balm to ease the ache in her heart.

CHAPTER TEN

THEY ALL ATE in the living room so that Celeste could remain lying on the sofa with her foot propped up. True to Rinna's word, Uma had wrapped a cloth around her ankle after applying the homemade poultice. Whatever the concoction was, it smelled heavenly. Miraculously, her foot started to feel better within minutes. Celeste didn't think it was the placebo effect. She could feel the swelling go down and the throbbing sensation had almost completely stopped. Between the filling meal and the relief from pain, she found herself drifting off into a comfortable sleep.

When she opened her eyes again, she was shocked that two hours had passed. She slowly roused herself to a seated position. Reid sat across from her at a wooden dining table, typing away at the keyboard of a laptop. He appeared to have showered and had changed into clean clothes. Oh, to be so lucky.

He glanced up when he realized she'd awakened. "You're up."

"It's dark out."

"That it is."

"Shouldn't our car have been here by now?"

"I asked for it to be delayed."

"Why?"

He shrugged. "You looked like you could use the rest. I didn't want to disturb you."

Great. Yet another misstep she could feel guilty about. "But I know you had to get back to the resort." And to finally meet whoever had been due to arrive earlier, she added silently.

Reid motioned to the computer in front of him. "It's okay. Theo was nice enough to lend me his laptop so I could get some stuff done remotely. How does your foot feel?"

Celeste wiggled her toes and moved her ankle from side to side. The pain had mostly subsided. Only a slight ache remained in the joint. "Much better. Rinna was right. Uma's potion has some sort of magical healing properties."

She huffed out a breath. "I feel so foolish for going and hurting myself like that. It must have been a terrible inconvenience for them to have to take care of me this whole time." And for him, too.

"Accidents happen. You're not at fault." He stood and walked over to stand in front of her.

"If you're up for it, I can call for the car to come for us."

Uma entered the room at that precise moment. "It's much too late to try to make that drive," the older woman argued. "You two stay here for the night. We have an extra room."

Reid gave Celeste a questioning look. He was waiting for her to make the decision. "I don't want to inconvenience anyone," Celeste said to the room in general.

Uma waved her hand in dismissal. "It's not a bother. Everything is ready for you. The bed stays made as we have overnight guests quite often. And the sofa down here is large and comfortable enough for you to sleep on, Reid."

Reid turned from the older woman to address Celeste. "Uma's offer makes sense. I'd feel better if you stayed completely off that ankle at least for the night. Also, I'd hate to make the driver leave his house this late just to drive us across the island and then have to drive back home again."

Well, how could she argue with any of that? She'd already been enough of a burden to the people currently under this roof. She certainly didn't want to further inconvenience the poor nameless driver.

"Thank you, Uma. You're far too kind," she told her, vowing to come up with a way to thank the woman at some future date. She'd never experienced such hospitality from strangers she'd met only hours before.

"That settles it then," Reid announced before turning to Uma. "We'll take you up on your generous offer. Thank you."

Uma patted his cheek and left the room. Celeste made an effort to get up off the coach. Reid was by her side in an instant. "Whoa there. What do you think you're doing?"

Embarrassingly enough, she needed to use the washroom, for one. "Uh, I could use to freshen up a little."

He wordlessly leaned down and lifted her off the sofa. It was hard not to savor the feel of being in his arms again, despite the circumstances that had led her there. He carried her to the nearest bathroom.

"Just holler when you're done."

Celeste shut the door and took a moment to study herself in the bathroom mirror. She looked as if she'd gone toe to toe with some kind of swamp creature. Her hair was a tangled mess, dark circles framed her eyes and her clothes were in a wrinkled state of disarray. Oh, yeah, compared to the gorgeous models and actresses Reid was used to dating, she would definitely fall far short.

With a resigned sigh, she cleaned up as best

she could, helping herself to some of the mouth-wash sitting on the bureau behind her.

She may not look great, but by the time she opened the door, she at least felt better. Reid remained in the same spot, waiting for her.

"All set?"

She nodded, trying to maintain her balance on the one foot. With what seemed to be little effort, he picked her up and carried her once more. "This can't be good for your back," she commented.

"You wound me. Are you questioning my masculine strength?"

She had to smile. "I wouldn't dream of it."

To her surprise, rather than plant her back on the sofa, he walked toward the front porch.

"Where are we going?"

"You'll see." Kicking the door open with his foot, he took her out onto the porch.

Once they stepped outside, the sight before her took her breath away. The lights that Theo had referred to earlier were now lit up. The whole garden looked like a magical holiday light display. Several Christmas trees, a few bushes decorated like presents, glowing lights along the path leading to the river. She couldn't help her squeal of delight at the festive scene.

"It's beautiful, Reid! I'm so glad I got to see it." She knew it was silly, but part of her was almost grateful for the accidental fall that had led her to be able to be here for this sight.

Reid set her down gently on one of the outdoor patio chairs then took a seat of his own. The night was balmy with just enough wind to offer a refreshing breeze once in a while. A silver-gray moon floated above them in a velvet navy blue sky. Celeste couldn't guess how long the two of them wordlessly sat there simply admiring the view.

Her awareness of the man next to her was near tangible, so she felt it instinctively when his mood seemed to shift. A tenseness suddenly appeared in the set of his shoulders. His chin hardened. His shoulders slumped ever so slightly, yet enough for Celeste to notice. No doubt he was thinking of all the responsibilities waiting for him back at the resort.

"I'm sorry we got stuck here. Due to my carelessness."

He turned to her, surprise flickering in his gaze. "Don't apologize, Celeste. You had an accident." He gestured around him. "Besides, how can I possibly be upset about spending time here amidst all this beauty and calm? I dare say I needed the peace and quiet for an evening."

Did that include spending time with her? Silly question.

"But you seem quite distracted. I imagine you're thinking of all you need to get done."

He shook his head, turned back to stare at the navy blue horizon in the distance. "Just thinking about a phone call I have to make when I get back."

"Must be some phone call." The tension was practically vibrating off his skin as he talked about it. "Business or personal? If you don't mind my asking."

He crossed his arms in front of his chest. "Both. That's the problem."

"Want to tell me about it?"

He shrugged. "I have the very unpleasant task of dispelling the notion my father has that he can retake control of Evanson Properties."

Celeste didn't know much about Reid's company, nothing beyond what she'd read in the business papers. But his statement confused her, based on those reports. "I don't understand. I thought the company was on the brink of bankruptcy until you took over as CEO and turned it around." He'd done so in an astonishingly brief period of time, too.

"He's not exactly thinking straight. His motivation has more to do with an outside party. A woman."

Understanding dawned. She'd also read about

the messy, bitter divorce of the elder Evansons. "I see."

He let out a grunt of a laugh. "My future stepmother has made it clear to him that she fell in love with a CEO, so she'd fully expected to marry a CEO."

"Sounds like a compromise might be difficult."

His eyebrows drew together. "Compromise?"

Celeste nodded. "There has to be a way for both you and your father to come to some kind of agreement."

He blinked at her. "Why would I bother? This is the man who let an uninformed, inexperienced outsider talk him into all sorts of bad investments. Everything from hiring social media influencers who simply took advantage of complimentary stays at our hotels, to investing in a failed music festival which resulted in countless lawsuits." He inhaled an agitated breath. "Lawsuits I'm still dealing with."

The underlying hurt in his tone was as clear as the flickering neon lights before them. His father's business failings were the least of the complicated scenario Reid was dealing with. No wonder he dreaded talking to the man.

"You feel betrayed," she supplied.

"How can I not? Evanson Properties was founded by my grandfather, it employs countless employees all over the globe. The Evanson name has been associated with luxury hotels for nearly a century. My father nearly destroyed all that with a few strokes of his pen. And for what? A midlife crisis?"

"But that's not all, is it?" she prompted.

"What else?"

Celeste bit the inside of her cheek. There was a chance she was overstepping here. But Reid was staring at her with expectation for an answer. "You also feel betrayed as his son."

Something seemed to have dislodged in his chest, some type of tight knot he hadn't even been aware of. He hadn't sat down and really discussed the disastrous events of the past couple of years or the hurtful actions of his father with anyone before this. He certainly wasn't about to burden his mother with any of it, she was a big part of the reason he'd worked so hard to rectify it all.

And his relationship with his closest male friend was far too strained and had been for the past three years. Unloading some of it simply by talking about it with Celeste felt like a bit of the burden being lifted off his shoulders.

You feel betrayed as his son.

He hadn't been able to come up with a response when she'd uttered those words. Her demeanor told him no response was needed.

Now they were both sitting in the balmy Caribbean air, enjoying a comfortable silence. He couldn't recall the last time he'd simply sat outside, chatting with someone. Someone who wasn't afraid to tell him what he needed to hear.

But it was getting late. And Celeste had had quite a day. Uma, Theo and Rinna had bidden them good-night several minutes ago and explained that the light display would turn off soon based on the timer system running it. Looked like the evening was coming to an end. And he'd already said more than he probably should have shared with her. He stood and stretched out his back.

"Guess we should head inside, huh?" Celeste asked.

"Guess so. Here, I'll help you upstairs to the spare bedroom."

Even in the relative darkness he could see her grimace. She didn't like being indebted to anyone. She might have read his thoughts based on her next statement. "I hate that you have to carry me, Reid. And I hate that you felt you needed to jump in after me when I fell." She inhaled deeply, her chest rising. "I'm not used to being dependent on anyone. It makes me uncomfortable. I'm afraid that's why I…lashed out…after my fall. I regret that. And I'd like to say I'm sorry for the way I behaved."

Huh. Reid couldn't recall the last time someone had directly come clean and apologized to him after making a mistake. Certainly not his father after the countless times he'd jeopardized the family business empire. And certainly not any of the women he'd dated in the recent past after a quarrel or spat. He'd always been the one to take responsibility and accept fault, regardless of whether it was deserved or not.

He checked his thoughts. It was way too late and the day had been way too long to become this pensive.

"Well, if it makes you feel better, you're probably one of the least dependent people I've ever come across," he told her with absolute sincerity. In fact, based on what she'd told him after the incident with the ATV, she'd made herself responsible not only for herself, but also for those she cared for. He hadn't known her that well three years ago, certainly hadn't been aware of the situation with her sister and mother. The knowledge now definitely shed some light on some of the mysteries he'd wondered about when it came to Celeste. In fact, if he'd been a betting man like his father, he would guess Celeste's family had been the real reason Jack had ultimately got cold feet over marrying her. He wasn't one to share. And he wasn't the type to appreciate a woman who came with that kind of baggage. Even a woman like Celeste.

Jack really could be incredibly selfish.

Reid couldn't help feeling somewhat sorry for him. The man had no idea what he'd had then foolishly lost. If Reid were in any kind of position to be with a woman like her, he'd hold on tight and refuse to let her go.

"Thank you for that," Celeste said. "It means a lot to hear you say so."

"You're welcome." Walking over to her chair, he cradled her in his arms and lifted her up. "Now I'm gonna get you to bed, beautiful."

He felt more than heard her sharp intake of breath, and couldn't decide whether she was reacting to the endearment or the loaded statement. He hadn't meant either, truth be told. He certainly hadn't meant to sound so provocative. "I'm sure you're ready to get some sleep," he quickly added.

Using his toe to nudge the door open, he carried her inside the house and up the stairs. He could get used to this, the feel of her in his arms. She was light and soft against his chest. Her shapely legs draped over his arms. The scent of her filling his senses. She belonged there, snuggled into him up against his chest.

Reid didn't bother with the light switch when

they reached the room, the moonlight and glow of the still-lit display outside afforded just enough light to see. Reid stepped over to the bed to gently set her down. But two things happened at once. First, the bed was much lower than he was used to. Second, the lights outside suddenly went out right at that very moment. Rather than gently set her down, Reid lost his footing and they both stumbled onto the mattress.

"We have to stop meeting like this," he quipped as they both landed unceremoniously onto the soft surface. Her lips were inches from his, he could feel her hot, sweet breath against his jaw. His skin felt afire everywhere her body touched his; the softness of her chest, her long legs up against his.

Her response was to tilt her face up toward his. Reid didn't even know who moved first. But suddenly he was tasting her, devouring her the way he'd so often imagined doing. He thrust his hands into her hair, pulled her tighter against him and deepened the kiss. She tasted like fruit and honey and enticing spice. She tasted like home.

Her hands found his shoulders, then moved over his biceps, toward his back. She wrapped her arms around his neck and deepened the kiss. But it wasn't enough. He would never get enough of her touch, the taste of her.

The sound of a door shutting from somewhere down the hall served as a warning bell. Though it hurt like a physical blow, he made himself break the kiss and pull away. He had to suck in a breath to try to steady his pounding pulse.

Celeste's cry of protest nearly undid him. But as much as he wanted to continue kissing and exploring her, this wasn't the time or the place.

One thing was unarguable. He wanted her. And she wanted him. There was no doubt in his mind judging by the way she'd reacted just now and the shallowness of her breathing as she stared up at him in confusion. He'd had to fight hard the strong urge to throw all care aside and simply join her where she lay on the bed.

Instead, he leaned down and dropped a gentle, soft kiss to her forehead. "Good night, Celeste." Then he forced himself to turn and walk away.

One and only one thought hammered his brain as he left the room to make his way down to the sofa on the first floor; he could make her forget she'd ever been committed to another man. Hell, he could make her forget that other man even existed.

There was no question of attraction. Not after what had just happened between them in that room and the way Celeste had melted in his arms. Under better circumstances, they could explore whatever this was between them and see where it might lead. If they were two completely different people, Reid would have no doubt in his mind about finding out once and for all.

No, the only question was whether he had any right to want her the way he did.

CHAPTER ELEVEN

THEIR TRIP TO the flower garden seemed like forever ago. Hard to believe only one day had passed. Celeste sank deeper into the Italian marble bath and took a deep breath. The hot water and luxurious fizziness of the scented bath bomb was doing wonders for her anxious nerves. But a dip in the bathtub could only do so much. She hadn't seen Reid all day yesterday once they'd arrived back at the resort, nor this morning or afternoon.

But she was due to spend the evening with him in a couple of short hours. The next item he had her writing up was a formal dinner cruise followed by live music and dancing aboard the boat.

What a fun, romantic evening it would have been if only it was all real. She had no idea what they would say to each other. The only words they'd spoken had been awkward and forced during their mostly silent drive back to the hotel yesterday morning after bidding Uma and her children goodbye. And then Reid had disappeared without a word to her except a brief text this morning confirming the time of the cruise. She'd been tempted to feign illness, to say that she wasn't up for it. But any fool would see right through that excuse.

Maybe he was avoiding her after what had happened in Uma's spare bedroom. Or perhaps he was busy with whoever had arrived that evening when the two of them couldn't return to the resort as expected. A pang of hurt she didn't want to identify as jealousy lodged in her chest.

The most probable explanation was that he was indeed avoiding her. He was no doubt embarrassed that things had gone so far between them that night. Heaven help her, she would have let things go even further if he hadn't suddenly stopped their kiss and walked out.

But he *had* walked out.

Reid had been the one to come to his senses. They had nothing in common, a shared brief past history which only complicated things further, and the chances that they would run into each other again once this trip was over were slim to none.

Unless, of course, she took him up on the free lifetime vacations he'd offered in return for her services. But she wouldn't. Her heart wouldn't be able to handle doing it. Seeing him every year, being tempted by a man she could never have.

A glance at the ornate clock on the wall above the sink counter told her she only had about half an hour left to get ready. With a sigh of regret, she stood and stepped out of the tub. There was no avoiding the inevitable. She could do this. She could dress the part, paste a fake smile on her face, and act like the all-business marketing professional that she was.

Toweling off, she walked over to the closet and removed the one formal dress that she'd packed. A silky black number that reached midthigh with red spaghetti straps and trim. Red leather high-heeled sandals and ruby earrings would complete the look. She'd included the outfit just in case when she'd packed, convinced she'd actually have no occasion to wear it.

If she'd only known.

About twenty minutes later, she was dressed and walking out the door of her suite to meet the man she'd somehow developed a devastatingly shocking attraction to.

This was a disaster in the making. The evening would no doubt be a lesson in self-torture. How was she going to playact the part of objective observer when the whole night all she'd be thinking about was how much she wanted him?

And heaven help her, she did want him. So much that she'd been aching inside ever since the other night. If she were honest with herself and looked deep within, she'd have to acknowledge something much more worrisome and disturbing: beyond the physical attraction, she'd developed feelings for him. Somehow, in the course of a few short days, she'd started falling for a man who was completely wrong for her. How many times in her life could she make the same mistake?

There was no denying that mistake when she reached the resort marina and found him waiting for her by the water. Celeste had to remind herself to breathe. Dressed in pressed dark pants and a midnight black fitted jacket with a collared shirt, he took her breath away. Against the backdrop of the luxury yacht and sparkling water, Reid could have been posing for a men's cologne ad. In fact, if she ever worked on a cologne campaign, this scene before her would serve as ample inspiration. She might find a way to use this image in the very project she was working on for the resort.

That's it, girl. Stay focused on the business aspect. Steady now.

Some protective instinct must have kicked into gear in her head. The survival skills she'd built and developed as an inner-city latchkey child were coming through for her as they so often had throughout her life. She could do this, she could get through this evening as an unemotional, unaffected, driven businesswoman who was simply attending this event as part of a job commitment.

And for all intents and purposes, the man standing before her was simply her boss.

Never mind that she wanted nothing more at this moment than to run into his arms.

Reid had to clench his fists by his sides in order to keep himself from pulling Celeste tight against him and into his arms when she reached his side. He'd come close to canceling this evening. That option would have been the wisest course of action. But he couldn't bring himself to do it. He needed this marketing project completed and he needed it completed successfully. Distractions and delays wouldn't do.

Or so he told himself. If pushed, he would have to concede that he hadn't called it off because he hadn't wanted to. He'd wanted to see her. Avoiding her this past day and a half had been nothing short of painful. And what did that say about the sad state he currently found himself in? He'd been missing a woman he had no claim to. A woman who would walk out of his life in a few short days and most likely never return.

Given the way she looked right now, he knew he wasn't likely to stop wanting what he couldn't have anytime soon. The silky black-and-red dress she wore complemented her ever-deepening tan. Strappy red high heeled shoes accented her shapely legs, she'd worn her hair down cascading like an ebony dark curtain over her satin smooth shoulders.

He swallowed hard.

"Hey there," she greeted him when she reached his side.

Somehow, he got his mouth to work. "Hey yourself." He handed her the rose he'd thought to pick up on his way. Fake date or not, he knew when an occasion called for a flower.

She seemed surprised as she took it and inhaled deeply of the petals. He wanted to do the same. Only he would prefer to nuzzle his face against the gentle curve of her neck and inhale deeply of her now oh-so-familiar scent.

"Thanks. This was very thoughtful."

"You're welcome," he replied, then motioned toward the boat behind them. "Shall we?"

Celeste took the hand he'd extended and followed him on board. A group of uniformed crew members greeted them and they made their way below deck. A few other couples were already seated at elegant, candlelit tables. Yet others strolled in behind them.

A white tuxedoed crew member led them to their table and pulled out their chairs.

"How's your foot?" Reid asked.

"Completely healed, it seems." She took a sip of her water. "Uma's poultice is a wonder drug. She should bottle that stuff and sell it worldwide."

"I might have to suggest that idea next time I'm at the flower garden." It occurred to him that on his next stop there he'd mostly likely be by himself. Or with Alex. He'd never be able to visit the place again without remembering the time he'd spent there with Celeste. Just one of the many marks she'd be leaving on him when she left the resort for good shortly.

The waiter reappeared with a fruity, frosted cocktail complete with a swirly straw and placed it in front of Celeste. "The bartender's specialty drink, miss. Please enjoy."

He placed a shorter glass full of amber liquid in front of Reid. Top-shelf Jamaican dark rum. "Your usual, sir."

Reid made a mental note to sip the drink much more slowly than usual tonight. He couldn't risk a repeat of the other night when he'd completely lost control and practically ravished Celeste in Uma's spare bedroom. Though he'd been stone-cold sober then. Still, he didn't want to take the chance of lessening his inhibitions in any way.

Celeste took a sip of her drink and closed her eyes in pleasure. "Mmm, this tastes heavenly. Definitely something to note when writing about this outing."

Good for her for keeping her mind on the task at hand, Reid thought. At least one of them had their head in the right place. So why was a small part of him just a touch disappointed?

"I've also got some great things to say about the light show at Uma's place," she continued, then looked down at her drink.

Their thoughts must have drifted in the same direction; what had transpired between them after they'd admired said light display that evening.

Reid cleared his throat, trying to summon exactly what he wanted to say. They had to acknowledge what had happened. Or this awkwardness was simply going to continue to grow.

"Celeste, I'm not sure where to begin, but maybe we should be talking—"

But she held an elegantly manicured hand up to stop him. "Please, Reid. If it's just as well with you, I'd like to focus on the here and now. I need to if I'm going to be effective in what I'm trying to do here tonight."

All right. He would have to respect her wishes if that's the way she wanted to play things.

He sighed and took the slightest sip of his drink. "If that's what you'd prefer. But we're going to run out of small talk at some point. And you can only do so much observation and analysis."

She leaned over the table, resting her elbows on the surface. "Let's discuss some fun things then," she suggested.

"Fun?"

She nodded with enthusiasm. "What does the man I'm working for do to have fun?"

The man she was working for. He wanted to correct her description of him. He'd been so much more than that the other night, hadn't he? But again, he would respect her wishes. He would play her small-talk game.

"What do you do outside of work, Reid? Do you have any hobbies? What happens when you finally have some free time and want to enjoy yourself?" She paused to take a sip of her drink. "And who do you spend that free time with?"

So, that's what this was about. She was asking if there was a woman in his life. Celeste wasn't as unaffected by their mutual attraction as she pretended. A selfish part of him couldn't help but feel pleased. And if that didn't make him self-centered, he didn't know what would.

He took another swig of his rum and focused

his gaze on her face. "Celeste, I believe you're asking me if I'm attached to anyone. Do I have that right?"

Celeste wanted to kick herself. She was usually much more subtle. In her defense, she hadn't realized that she planned to ask him that question. It had just come blurting out of her lips. Now it was too late to take it back.

"Just trying to learn more about you, that's all."

He flashed her a knowing smile. "All right, I'll bite," he stated. "I don't have much time for hobbies. But when I can get away, I enjoy a good getaway to the mountains for downhill skiing. In warmer climates, I'm an avid scuba enthusiast. Been certified since my teens. It's one of the reasons I started looking into the Caribbean as an investment opportunity."

So he was going to start with the less loaded questions. Then again, maybe he wouldn't answer her last question at all. Served her right. His personal life was none of her business, not really.

What did it matter that they'd lost control with each other on a couple different occasions? They'd simply both been carried away by the romantic setting and the adrenaline rush afforded by all the activities they'd done together. The strong possibility was that he probably had several girlfriends. He probably dated someone different in every city he traveled to. That was the impression she'd first gotten of him when they'd met three years ago at Jack's introduction. As a matter of fact, she distinctly remembered a conversation about which lucky lady Reid would bring to the wedding as his companion. Her bridesmaids had certainly fallen over each other trying to get his attention. She'd thought it rather amusing at the time. Not so much now. Now that he could also count her as one of the many females who had a thing for him.

They were interrupted by another server who appeared with a platter of cold shellfish. Everything from oysters, to clams, to chilled lobster garnished with lemons and capers sat on a bed of ice. Simultaneously, a sommelier appeared with a bottle of red wine and handed the cork to Reid. He simply nodded at the man after taking a small sniff. Another bottle of white wine was also placed alongside the table in a standing silver bucket sweaty with condensation.

Good thing she hadn't eaten all day. This was only the first course. Not that she had much of an appetite. Her frazzled nerves were wreaking havoc on her stomach.

Think of this as a straightforward business meeting.

Her own words mocked her. The way Reid looked in his suit and the romantic mood of the setting made that darn near impossible.

She vowed to try. "I've never been scuba diving," she said, resuming their conversation after the servers had left. "I do ski occasionally. Nothing more than bunny trails. That's all I have the courage or the balance for, I'm afraid. I'm not much of an athlete." Unlike him.

His gaze dropped to her shoulders then traveled down and Celeste had to suppress a shiver of awareness. "If you don't mind my saying," he began. "You're clearly quite fit."

It was downright silly to feel as giddy as she did about that compliment.

"I do a lot of yoga. It helps center me. I started in college." Thank goodness she had. Between the stress of her job, the long hours, and the continuous mess that was her family life, she needed the release and quiet peacefulness of the practice.

"Makes sense." Reid offered her one of the lobster tails. "I've never tried it, but I hear some of the poses can be very physically demanding."

"Oh, yes. Definitely. Some of the more challenging ones can have me breathless with my muscles screaming and sweat pouring over my skin while I hold the pose."

"Sounds athletic to me."

She shrugged. "I guess."

He leaned back in his chair, studied her. "You do that a lot, don't you?"

"Do what?"

"Discount yourself. What you're capable of."

His statement surprised her. "I—I didn't realize I did."

"You were certain climbing the falls was going to be too much for you. Yet you handled it just fine."

"I had you there to guide and catch me."

He ignored that. "And the way you disparaged your karaoke performance."

Now he had to be teasing her. "Do you blame me? I sounded horrible. Pitchy and completely off key."

"Is that your takeaway from that night?"

"It's the truth! Please don't pretend I have any talent whatsoever as a singer."

"No. I won't."

She had to laugh at that quick response acknowledging her lack of singing ability. "Thank you."

"Does that mean you should never sing karaoke?" he asked with all seriousness. Celeste was beginning to wonder if this might be one of the most vexing conversations she'd ever had. To top it off, they were supposed to be talking about *him*.

"I dunno. I might say that's exactly what it means."

"You'd be wrong. You may be bad at singing. But you're great at karaoke."

Okay. Now he was making zero sense. "Uh… Come again?"

"You were magnificent up there when we sang together," he declared.

Magnificent? "Um… I was?"

He nodded with zero hesitation.

"How do you figure?"

"You were engaging and endearing, despite being scared out of your mind. Most important, you had the crowd entertained. Off key or not, they were with you through the whole song, some singing along. Others simply bouncing to the beat of the song."

Huh. Had that really been the way that whole scene had played out? She'd been so nervous, all she'd thought about was getting through the song and fleeing off the stage.

"I was?" she stammered, completely shocked at what he was telling her.

"Yes. You were. Everyone who witnessed it saw how amazing you were that night. Everyone but you."

CHAPTER TWELVE

HE'D IMPLIED THAT he found her amazing. Celeste couldn't seem to get that thought out of her head. They'd finished their dinner of salt fish and grilled vegetables moments ago and were now on the upper deck of the boat admiring the star-filled night sky and the tranquility of the Caribbean waters as they sailed over the surface.

For a conversation that had started out all about Reid, he'd certainly given her a lot to think of about herself. All her life she'd been told that she wasn't enough, that she had to try harder, be better, simply to be enough. Her mother certainly found her lacking. As did her younger sister. Her fiancé had left her emotionally bruised and publicly humiliated.

Yet here was this charming, enigmatic man trying to tell her the exact opposite—that she didn't give herself enough credit.

They'd carried their wine goblets up with them and Celeste took a sip of her drink as she admired the view. The band due to perform was setting up a few feet away toward the stern as she and Reid stood portside. They couldn't have asked for a more perfect evening for a dinner cruise. She couldn't deny that she was enjoying herself. Despite the somewhat awkward start to the evening, she and Reid had managed to lapse into an easy state of camaraderie and friendly conversation. But she couldn't get some of the things he'd just said about her out of her mind.

"You appear to have drifted off. Penny for your thoughts?" he asked, not looking away from the horizon.

Celeste gave a small shake of her head. "Just admiring the beautiful evening, I guess."

It occurred to her that he still hadn't answered her earlier question. This time, she'd take a different approach. "You were worried the other night about missing someone who was due to fly onto the island," she ventured. "Were they upset that you weren't there to greet them when they arrived?"

Perfectly innocent question. But maybe it would give her some kind of hint as to his relationship status. But Reid only shook his head. "No, they were perfectly understanding."

That told her absolutely nothing about who he was supposed to meet that night. Maybe a more direct approach was necessary after all.

Though heaven knew she should just drop the entire matter altogether. But she couldn't seem to let it go.

Reid gave her a chance at an opening with his next question. "So, tell me. Is there no one at home upset that you aren't there with them to celebrate the holidays?"

"Not really. What about you? Is anyone unhappy that you're here, essentially working through the holidays?"

He smiled at her. "You first. I don't consider 'not really' much of an answer."

She blew out a long sigh. "Yes. My mother and sister are upset that I left the city for the holidays. But they're upset for all the wrong reasons." Celeste fought to find the exact right way to explain. She didn't particularly want to get into the whole matter of her family and all their dysfunction. It would only spoil the evening.

"I don't understand," Reid prompted.

"Christmas wasn't particularly a joyous occasion for me as a child. I grew up with a single mother who couldn't always make ends meet. Most years, she would have to work over the holiday, she usually waitressed. And I'd end up having to babysit my younger sister, who was usually upset and cranky that Mommy was gone and she was stuck at home with just her sister. Not much celebrating happened."

He'd turned to face her fully, listening intently to her every word.

"So, you see," she continued. "Christmastime wasn't exactly festive to begin with."

"And then your Christmas wedding happened," he supplied for her.

"Or didn't happen, to be more accurate. There's really nothing I find celebratory about it. Better to just take off for several days of fun and sun."

He reached for her hand over the railing, held it gently in his. "I'm sorry, Celeste. You didn't deserve that. Any of it."

Oh, no, they were not going to discuss Jack. Not here, not now. "Don't be!" she quickly countered before things headed in that direction. "I'd say I'm lucky. Nothing wrong with spending the holidays in paradise on a tropical island."

He looked less than convinced but didn't push. "Your turn," she prompted.

Reid let go of her hand and took a sip of his wine. Was it wrong that she wanted to reach for him again?

"No. My parents split wasn't terribly amicable. My mother's active with a lot of charities that ramp up their activity during the holiday season. And my father is in Aspen currently to spend the holidays skiing with his newly found love, a woman he left his wife of thirty years for."

"I see," was all Celeste could manage in response. For all the people the world over who looked forward to Christmas every year, there had to be just as many who dreaded it. "I'm sorry too, Reid."

He gave a small shrug. "No need. I have plenty that keeps me occupied during the holidays. The hospitality industry doesn't exactly slow down at Christmas. If anything, things are even busier. Then there's all the effort still required to clean up the mess made by Father's recent business decisions." He lifted his glass in mock salute before taking a long swig.

The resentment in Reid's voice was as clear as the starry sky above them.

"So, I guess you and I are a lot alike in many regards," he added, taking another sip of cabernet.

"How so?"

He turned to her once more. "Isn't it obvious? It appears neither one of us will be reveling in yuletide cheer anytime soon."

This conversation was becoming way too heavy. Reid shook off the melancholy that suddenly threatened the atmosphere between him and Celeste. He took the opportunity of a passing waiter to unburden them of their now empty wineglasses. Enough deep talk for now.

The band had finished setting up and began

to play a reggae version of "Holly Jolly Christmas." The happy tune immediately lured several couples up and onto the dance floor.

"You think your foot might be up to a dance?" he asked Celeste.

At her somewhat hesitant nod, he gently took her by the elbow and they joined the other dancers. The tempo was just bouncy enough that they could sway easily to the beat. "I see you have yet another talent, Mr. Evanson. Consider me impressed with your footwork."

"Mother insisted on years of dance lessons. Said I needed to be cultured," he answered over the loud music. "You're not so bad yourself."

He couldn't recall going dancing with a woman and actually enjoying himself this much. Celeste seemed to be able to bring a level of energy and fun to whatever she was doing. It was infectious. The dance floor grew more and more crowded as the band started the next number. Celeste was a natural, her movements fluid and in tune with the music. He noticed several pairs of appreciative male eyes on her and reflexively stepped closer. Their bodies brushed against each other as they both moved. Hot, sharp need seared through him every time they made contact. When the band launched into a much slower song, Reid didn't give himself a chance to think. Her wrapped his arms around her and pulled her tight up against him. She didn't protest or make any effort to pull away. Thank the gods for he wasn't sure if he'd be able to let her go.

One of the band members began to speak through the mike over the music. "We're going to make sure everyone has a good time tonight," he announced to responding applause and cheers. He went on, "I hear there are a lot of couples here celebrating."

More cheers sounded. "Raise your hands if you're here to celebrate an anniversary."

Several sets of hands went up.

"How many of you are here on your honeymoon?" The bandmate asked.

Another round of hands responded along with raucous cheers, including from the young blonde woman and her companion who were dancing right next to them.

Celeste gave the couple a warm smile. "Congratulations," she said over all the noise around them.

"Thank you!" The woman responded with a grin. "We got married two days ago." She wagged a finger between him and Celeste. "How long have you two been together?"

"Oh, we're not—" Celeste began.

Reid decided to spare her the awkwardness. "We've known each other for about three years," he answered truthfully. The lady didn't need to know the details.

"That's lovely!" the other woman declared. "We only met last year. But it was love at first sight, you know? We've been inseparable ever since. When it's the right person, you just know. All the signs are there. I had no doubt he's the man I'm meant to spend my life with the moment I met him."

Her spouse nodded enthusiastically in agreement next to her as they continued to dance.

"That's really wonderful," Celeste said, her tone wistful enough that Reid instinctively pulled her closer against him.

"Thanks! I hope we're having as much fun in three years as you two are together."

Celeste seemed to deflate in his arms. He figured she could use a drink. "Why don't we head below deck for some refreshments?" he suggested.

She didn't hesitate, following him off the dance floor and to the bar down the starboard steps. He ordered them more wine once they were seated on the bar stools. But once their glasses arrived, Celeste didn't so much as take a sip. She merely rubbed her finger around the rim, deep in thought.

Reid cursed the loss of the easy companionship they'd been enjoying before running into the newlyweds. He could only guess what Celeste was thinking. She was wondering if she'd ever have what that couple had. If she'd experience the thrill of a honeymoon, or dancing with her new husband above deck aboard a dinner boat cruising over the Caribbean waters.

It was the strangest thing, but he was thinking along those same lines for himself. Definitely not something he'd ever considered before. He shook off the useless thoughts. He already had his hands more than full. Between the family holdings and his father's self-destructive behavior, Reid didn't have it in him to commit to any other kind of relationship.

His gaze fell on the woman sitting next to him.

No. He couldn't even go there, couldn't allow himself to think those thoughts. Celeste had been hurt enough in her lifetime. The last thing she needed was someone like him toying with her affections further.

But they had the rest of this trip. At the least, they had the rest of tonight. There was nothing wrong with enjoying each other's company.

Though Celeste looked far from joyful at the moment. He would have to do something about that. He couldn't have her this forlorn. The evening was much too beautiful to let it go to waste. They were the only people downstairs at the bar, with everyone else still at the dance party above.

He stood and took her by the hand. "Here, follow me." Acknowledging the sole bartender, he walked her behind the bar and led her to the kitchen area behind it. Several cooks and servers waved as they entered. Reid walked over to the freezer in the center of the room and reached inside.

Celeste blinked at the carton he'd pulled out. "Ice cream?"

"Chocolate."

Her confusion grew into a wide smile. "Where do we find spoons?"

Five minutes later they stood at the hull of the boat with his jacket thrown over Celeste's shoulders and the wind blowing around them, spooning chocolate ice cream straight out of its container.

She didn't want the night to end. And it was just silly to think that way. It wasn't as if she and Reid were walking back to her room after any kind of real date. Foolish, really.

Reid's suit jacket still hung over her shoulders, the smell of him enveloping her, reminding her of the way it had felt to be in his arms on the dance floor. Not to mention, all those other times when they'd been alone.

A shiver ran over her skin. He must have noticed. "Are you still cold? I can call for a beach cart to drive you back to your room," he offered.

No. That wasn't what she wanted. She wanted to continue walking with him, to delay the inevitable. When they would part for the night. What then? Reid didn't mention any other activity he wanted her to attend, no other excursions were planned. For all she knew, this was it.

There would be no more opportunities to spend any time alone with him. Celeste felt an ache of pain in the center of her chest.

"I'm actually enjoying the night air. Thank you for walking me back."

"What kind of gentleman would I be if I left you to head back to your suite by yourself?"

"The kind that serves a girl chocolate ice cream on the hull of a boat during a dinner cruise?"

He laughed at that. The rest of their stroll continued on in pleasant silence, the night air balmy and comfortable. Celeste indulged in a slight fantasy and just let herself pretend. Just for these few short moments, she would make believe that she had what that couple on that boat had. That she'd found the man she was meant to be with and had known right away. And that, fanciful as it was, Reid happened to be that man.

Never mind that her reality was the complete opposite. By contrast, the one time she'd been engaged, it had been a mistake of epic proportions. And with Reid… She sighed. She honestly didn't know the true reality when it came to Reid. He was obviously attracted to her. But what did that mean when he was so quick to step back from her before things could go anywhere? The answer should be obvious, she figured. He knew they had no business being together, so he wasn't going to let things get too far. Wise of him. Unlike her, he was thinking straight.

Maybe she was done with having to do the wise thing, though. Maybe this one time she wanted more. Even if it was just temporary. It might shatter her inside afterward when it all ended and she had to leave, but in her heart she knew it would be worth it.

She just had to know. Without giving herself a chance to think, she blurted out one of the questions that had been on her mind. "I know it's getting late. Do you have to rush to get back? Is someone waiting for you?"

He turned and lifted an eyebrow in question. "What?"

"You were due to meet someone that day when we got stranded at the flower garden. You appeared upset to have to miss them. Are they waiting for you right now?"

The eyebrow lifted ever so higher. "My spirits supplier?"

She clasped a hand to her mouth. "Oh. You were due to meet your spirits supplier that night?"

He nodded once. "That's right. Who did you think it might have been?"

Celeste felt heat rush to her cheeks. Well, at least now she knew. And she couldn't help the sense of relief and giddiness that washed over her at the newfound knowledge. But it had all come at a price. Reid was on to her. He'd be stupid not to have figured out what she was getting at.

They'd reached her building and made their way to her door on the second floor. Celeste turned to face him, not even sure what she was going to say. The only thing she was certain of was that she wasn't ready to walk through that door just yet.

Her heart hammered in her chest as Reid stepped closer to her. She felt the wooden door up against her back as the warmth of his body seeped into the front of hers.

"Why did you want to know?" he asked on a strained whisper.

Her nerves completely on edge and with Reid standing so close, it was hard to think of an answer. The truth. She would go with the truth. She was done with the pretenses. "I think you know why."

"Spell it out for me, Celeste. I don't want to jump to any conclusions here."

Celeste sucked in a deep breath for courage. She was really doing this. "Go ahead and jump. You'd be correct."

Heat darkened his eyes and he visibly stiffened.

And then she couldn't take it anymore. Moving fully up against him, she slid her arms around his neck and brought her face up to his.

It was all the invitation he needed.

He hauled her tight into him and crushed his mouth to hers. He tasted of wine and chocolate and pure, unfiltered male. It was a taste she would never get enough of. The scent of him rushed her senses. His hands moved over her hips and up to her rib cage. All the while, his mouth continued pleasuring her lips, his kiss growing deeper.

"Reid, yes," she managed to whisper against his mouth.

She'd never been so wanton, so in need. But that was the only way to describe the state she was in. She *needed* this man. She needed his arms around her, and to have him hold her all night. And there was no reason not to give in to that primal desire.

Not for this one night, anyway.

Morning would come soon enough.

CHAPTER THIRTEEN

HE WAS GONE.

Celeste could feel his absence without even having to open her eyes. He must have left her bed in the middle of the night. Tears formed behind her lids and she opened them slowly to glance at the bedside clock. Just past midnight. There was no way she would be getting any sleep. Her body felt languid, the heat of Reid's touch still lingered on her skin. He'd brought her to a feeling of euphoria she'd never experienced before.

It was highly unlikely she would ever experience it again. Her eyes stung further before she shoved the sorrow aside. She was a big girl; she'd made her decision and would learn to live with it somehow.

A shadow moved outside on her balcony.

Celeste rubbed her eyes to make sure she wasn't seeing things. A surge of hope shot through her chest when she looked again. Reid hadn't left, he was standing on her balcony, arms draped over the railing, staring out at the ocean in the distance. He was still here. But everything about his stance told her that something was off.

Celeste stood and walked to the closet where the terry cloth robe hung on a hanger. Throwing it on, she took a deep breath. If she was smart, she'd go back to bed and feign that she was still asleep. But something about the rigid set to Reid's back, the way his head hung forward, called to her. She just had to hope he wanted her to go to him right now.

Well, she was about to find out.

Sliding the glass door open slowly, she stepped out onto the concrete in her bare feet.

"Hey, there," she said softly.

He didn't turn to her. "Sorry if I woke you."

"I awoke on my own. Weren't you able to sleep, either?"

He shook his head. "Happens sometimes."

"I thought at first that you'd left."

"Would you like me to?"

Her answer was immediate. "No! Don't." *Please stay*, she added silently, hating herself for the despair flooding her insides at the threat of him walking out right now.

He simply shrugged. "Okay."

Okay? That was all he was going to say?

She sucked in a breath. "Would you like to be alone?"

He remained silent so long that Celeste was convinced he wasn't going to answer her. Which was answer enough in itself, she figured. But then he finally turned to her, reached for her hands.

"No. I've been alone long enough. Stay with me."

She wouldn't allow herself to look too deeply into his words. They'd just been intimate with each other, as close as two people could get. And heaven help her, she only wanted desperately to be back in his arms again, snuggled up against him in her bed. The next time she woke up, she wanted to be nestled in his embrace with his warmth surrounding her body.

Right now, she stepped into his open arms and let him hold her. After several moments, he exhaled deeply and turned her to face the ocean, her back up against his front.

She could feel his chest rise and fall with each breath he took. His strong, muscular arms held her tightly around her waist.

"It's beautiful out there, isn't it?" he asked, his breath hot up against her ear.

She nodded under his chin. "The whole resort is a sight to behold. You've really done well here, Reid."

He continued, "It's times like this when I wish I could simply take it all in and just enjoy this place. Rather than worry about how it's run. Or if we'll turn enough of a profit. It's all just so new."

He had a huge burden on his shoulders, she knew. She hadn't realized just how heavily it all must have weighed on him.

"I wish there was a way I could help."

"You are helping. You're helping me put the marketing plan together to help sell this place. I couldn't have asked for a better contractor."

Celeste tried not to bristle at the reminder that she was essentially his temporary employee. He had to see her as more than that after what they'd just shared.

Or was it simply wishful thinking on her part to think so?

"I'll do my best, Reid. But something tells me you would have figured out the marketing approach with or without me."

He turned her to face him then, dropped a soft kiss along the base of her neck. Red-hot desire had her shuddering all over. It was quite a marvel how the smallest peck of a kiss from him could make her insides burn with want.

"I'm glad it was with you," he said then took her lips in a hungry kiss. "So very glad."

Any thought of profits or marketing strategies completely fled her mind as soon as his lips touched hers. Her only focus was the man holding her, kissing her, making her *want*. Her arms instantly went around his neck as his hands found her skin underneath the robe.

The next instant she was lifted off her feet and carried inside.

Where he set her further aflame.

Reid woke up to find Celeste sprawled over his chest. She was still sound asleep. Her breath was hot against his chest, hair spread out fanlike over his skin. He took the opportunity to run his fingers over their silken strands, remembering the way he'd thrust his hands through them last night and the way she'd melted in his arms over and over again.

Morning had come all too soon. A glance at the tableside clock told him that it was much later than he usually started the day. Alex was probably wondering where he was.

Yep, reality had dawned just as clearly as the morning sun. He couldn't shove it aside any longer. Unwilling to let her go just yet, he pulled Celeste ever so slightly up against him. They would have some talking to do later. Though he had no real idea where he would start the conversation. He couldn't risk mucking it all up by trying before he'd even figured things out.

He had nothing to offer her. His world was hotels and resorts and meetings and investments. And somehow consoling his betrayed mother. Not to mention preparing for the fight he was certain was coming from his father. Dale Evanson wanted to regain control of the company he'd almost run into the ground. And he had enough cronies on the board who were ready to help him get what he was after.

A woman like Celeste had no room in her life for so many complications. Especially when she had enough of her own to contend with. Oh, and there was that whole former-fiancée-of-a-good-friend thing hanging above their heads, as well. He couldn't let himself forget that.

Yeah, reality could land a real kick to the gut sometimes.

Reid swore softly under his breath and made an effort to gently remove himself from bed without rousing her. She stirred but didn't open her eyes. It took a few more tries before he was able to disengage out of their embrace. He reached for his shirt and pants lying over the back of the leather chair. He had to go start his day. He would have to leave her a note or try calling her later.

But there would be no need to do either of

those things. Celeste slowly opened her eyes and sat halfway up. She looked so alluring with her hair in complete disarray and her lips still swollen from his kisses. He could see the minor redness on her shoulders and around her chest where he'd rubbed his beard over her skin. He had to close his eyes to keep from crawling back into bed and joining her once more.

"You're up."

He nodded. "I have to get going. There's a lot happening today." *On and off the resort*, he added under his breath.

"Does that mean breakfast together is out of the question?" The look of longing in her eyes nearly undid him. He had to hold firm.

"I'm afraid so. I have one meeting after another." Starting with the business partner who was probably wondering where the devil he was at this very moment.

"I see."

He leaned over the bed, brushed a soft kiss across her temple. "You go back to sleep. No need for both of us to leave the warmth and comfort of the bed."

"It's not quite as warm anymore," she countered.

Reid ignored that, just turned to throw his pants on. Then he pulled his shirt over his shoulders. He had to turn away, if he continued looking at the enticing picture she made—with the sheet pulled up over the roundness of her breasts—he wasn't sure how much resolve he could muster. He wasn't made of stone, after all.

"I have to get you my written recommendations," Celeste said behind him as he sat in the chair to tie his shoes. "I've already got most of it written up on my tablet. I can use the business office to get it all printed once I finish."

"No need to do that," Reid threw over his shoulder. "Would you mind sending it via text? As an attachment. I'll look at it when I get a chance."

She sat studying him as he finished the last knot and stood. "Sure. I can do that," she answered.

"Thanks. I'm really looking forward to seeing what you have to say."

"Reid…"

"Yes?"

She opened her mouth but shut it again without speaking. Instead, she dropped back onto the pillow behind her and flung her arm over her face. "Never mind. It's not important."

Reid fought the urge to go to her side and indulge in another kiss, this time to her lips. But it would be dangerous to risk tasting her again. The sooner he walked out of this room, the better for both of them.

"Bye, sweetheart," he said and pulled the door open.

She didn't answer before he walked out.

She had no one but herself to blame.

Celeste turned the nozzle of the shower to the very end of the hot setting, allowing the punishing heat of the water to wash over her until she could stand it no longer. It did nothing to scorch away her internal anguish. What had she been expecting? To spend the day with Reid holding hands and walking along the beach? She'd understood last night exactly what she was getting into. The fact that she was hurt and disappointed by the way he'd left this morning was no one's fault but her own.

She'd been naive, fooling no one except herself. She knew how ill-equipped she was for meaningless flings. She'd gone ahead and spent the night with Reid anyway. Worse yet, she'd fooled herself into thinking she could somehow conveniently forget that she'd fallen for him. It had only been a few days since she'd arrived on the island and run into him again. But it was like the newlywed on the dinner cruise had said last night—when you're with the right person, you just know.

Celeste just knew.

Though they hadn't been on the best of terms

three years ago when she'd first met him, she'd
noted Reid's determination and quiet strength.
How hard he seemed to work as chairman of his
family business. He'd always been a good friend
to Jack, coming through for him with countless
errands to help with the responsibilities of the
would-be groom. Of all Jack's friends, it was
only Reid whom she'd grown to admire.

And the time she'd spent with him these past
few days had grown that admiration into so
much more. Celeste bit back a sob.

She stayed under the spray until the water
turned cold and her skin started to prune. Then
she made herself take a deep breath and shake
off the useless, defeatist thoughts. Celeste Frajedi had learned long ago that the best way to
overcome any stumble or setback was to keep
busy and work hard. Stepping out of the stall,
she toweled off, threw on shorts and a tank top,
then ordered coffee and breakfast from room
service. Then she pulled up her tablet and got to
work. She had a marketing report to complete.

CHAPTER FOURTEEN

HER SCRAMBLED EGGS sat cold and untouched an
hour later when Celeste started putting the final
touches to her write-up. Though the entire pot
of coffee was gone. The next pot she ordered
could be enjoyed relaxing on the balcony and
watching the beach scene outside, now that she
had the file mostly completed. And she'd done
a good job with it too, if she did say so herself.
There was a part of the report that could prove
risky. A professional should never allow personal feelings to affect a business project, but
she'd decided to take the chance. There wasn't
much left to lose.

The ring of her cell phone pulled her focus.
Reid.

Her hand immediately reached for the device.
Without stopping to glance at the screen, she
immediately clicked the answer button, didn't
even care how anxious she'd appear at having
answered so quickly.

She was wrong. The voice that greeted her over the line was a husky feminine one. The first words spoken were slurred.

"Hope you're having fun lying on the beach while the rest of us are stuck here."

Her mother.

Celeste tried to clamp down on the alarm rising within her core. This was twice in a matter of days. Wendy's problems appeared to be escalating. So far, this was turning into one sucker punch of a day.

"Hello, Mother. Is something the matter back at home?"

Her mother grunted in clear disgust. "Better believe there is."

An icicle of fear dropped into Celeste's stomach. "Is everything okay with the baby? What is it?"

"The baby's fine," her mother huffed. Celeste allowed herself a moment of relief before her mother continued. "Your sister needs to start looking for another job, ya know."

Celeste grasped for patience. What she did know for certain was that Tara wasn't in any rush to do any kind of job search. Especially now, mere days away from Christmas. "Mother, please tell me why you're calling. You said something was wrong."

"I'll have you know they're threatening to

shut off my power. It's below freezing here. Not like that sunny, warm place you're at. And they're gonna try to cut my heat off."

Alarm tightened Celeste's muscles. "What? Why?"

"I don't know. They're saying the bill wasn't paid."

"Are they saying that because it's true? Did you neglect to pay the bill?"

"I don't remember."

"Just send the check out now. Pay it as soon as you can."

"I got nothing to pay it with, do I?"

Celeste rubbed a weary hand over her forehead. Her mother's account must be seriously overdue for the utility to be threatening to shut off supply. Which meant Wendy hadn't paid the bill for several months.

"Momma, I deposited more than enough money in your account to cover all the expenses and utilities." And she'd done so consistently every month. "Why didn't you pay the bill?"

A muffled sound echoed from the tiny speaker. Was that a sob? Celeste's earlier alarm turned into an icy brick of fear in the pit of her stomach. "I kept trying to win the money, Celeste," Wendy said on a loud hiccup. "And I came so close, but then the table would turn the other way." There was no doubt now that Wendy was indeed crying.

"Have you been gambling?"

Another hiccup followed by a sniffle. "I was just tryin' a get some money to buy the baby some extra-special Christmas presents. Wanted to do it on my own, without help from nobody."

Celeste leaned back in her chair, her surprise almost too much to contain. Her mother had actually wanted to feel the pride of getting her first grandchild a holiday gift without asking for money from anyone else. Mainly her.

Celeste couldn't help but feel touched. But Wendy had gone about it in an oh-so-wrong way.

One thing was clear. Her mother needed to get help. It couldn't be put off any longer. Not only did her occasional alcohol benders seem to be growing more frequent, she now ran the very real risk of acquiring a gambling addiction, too.

"Mother, stop crying. I'll take care of the electricity bill, okay?"

"Th-thank you," Wendy was no longer trying to hold back the wails. "I didn't want to freeze."

"You won't. And we'll be sure to get Nat a wonderful present when I get back, okay? But you have to stop trying to win the money."

"Okay."

"Promise me, Mother."

"I promise," Wendy answered, and another loud sniffle followed.

Celeste squeezed her eyes shut and counted her breath for several beats after her mother hung up. It took some time, but finally her pulse started to slow and some of the tension left her midsection. She would need a full and long meditation session soon to try to take the edge off her frayed emotions. Given her day already, the session would have to be a marathon one.

She had so much to take care of once she returned to New York City.

But first things first. Saving the document she was working on, she switched browsers and called up her mother's electricity bill. The sum in arrears made her gasp. It was a wonder the electricity company hadn't shut her off already. With resignation and sadness, Celeste transferred the amount out of her own checking account to cover the debt.

This was her truth. Her reality.

Incidents like this were the reason she shouldn't have forgotten herself last night. Worse, they were the reason she should have never let herself fall for a man like Reid Evanson in the first place. Why hadn't she learned her lesson the first time?

For his reality was so very different from the one she lived in.

* * *

Alex made a show of glancing at his watch when Reid finally made it into the office later that morning. Reid braced himself for the inevitable ribbing that was sure to be headed his way.

"Yeah. I know I'm late, partner. How about giving me some slack this one time, huh?" he asked, his arms spread out and his palms up.

Alex rubbed his jaw. The serious playacting he was attempting was severely undercut by the quiver of a smile at the corners of his mouth. "I don't know, man. I mean, you've been the one out enjoying yourself on all these various excursions with a beautiful woman by your side who you say is 'helping you.'" He added air quotes with his fingers as he spoke the last two words.

Reid had to groan out loud at the mention of Celeste. Alex noticed, of course. He immediately turned serious.

"What's happened?"

He really didn't want to get into any of this. Not ever. He didn't want to discuss Celeste at all. In fact, he didn't even want to think about her. Because doing that would undoubtedly tempt him to seek her out and drag her back to her room where they could run a replay of last night.

Just. Stop.

It was a risk he couldn't take.

"Nothing happened," he fibbed to his business partner. "I just overslept." That part was at least the truth.

Alex's eyes narrowed on him, clearly questioning whether to accept his answer as the whole truth. Reid knew he was too sharp and would see through it without effort. He was right. "I can't recall another time you've ever overslept."

"It was bound to happen sometime."

Alex gave a slight shrug of his shoulder. "Suit yourself. Don't tell me, then."

"What did I miss around here?" Reid asked, in a blatantly obvious move to change the subject.

Luckily, Alex was going to play along. "The usual," he answered. "A few minor guest complaints. The tennis pro asked that the courts be redone. And we're running low on chardonnay."

Reid gave him a nod. "Got it. I'll go make some phone calls." He pivoted toward his office.

"And then there's your father," Alex called out after him.

Reid stopped in his tracks and turned back to face his friend. "What about him?"

"He's been calling the office all morning. Says he got tired of leaving you messages on your cell just to have you ignore him."

Of course his father would say that. The truth

was, Reid had given him every opportunity to change the course of the disastrous path they currently found themselves on.

"How's that whole thing going anyway?" Alex asked.

"About as well as can be expected. He wants full control of the company back." What made it so much worse was that Reid knew his father was ready to retire. The only reason he was doing this was to please his new bride-to-be.

"Any chance of that happening?" Alex wanted to know.

Reid shrugged. "He has some cronies on the board who are ready to vote as he wants." Reid would risk an all-out battle before he let that vote go his father's way—if it ever came to a vote.

Alex let out a low whistle. "Hostile take-over attempts can be brutal under any circumstances."

"Let alone amongst family," Reid finished his thought for him.

"I'm here if you want to talk," Alex said to his back as Reid walked into his office.

Once there, with the door shut, he finally let out the full brunt of the frustration he'd been feeling since leaving Celeste's bed this morning, by launching his priceless signed Red Sox vintage baseball across the room. It hit the wall with a loud thud and sent chips of paint flying.

Great. One more thing to have to fix. This time, he'd done it to himself.

If Alex heard the noise outside in the foyer, he was too astute to knock and ask him about it. Not that he ever actually knocked.

The angry calls from his father served as a reminder that he was right to leave Celeste this morning without lingering any further the way he'd wanted to. He'd so badly wanted to. The right thing to do was to leave her alone.

It wouldn't be easy, and it would take a great deal of effort, but eventually, he might even stop thinking about the way she'd felt in his arms last night.

An internal voice immediately mocked him. *Yeah, right.* He'd be thinking about her touch for the rest of his natural life. He could only hope to stop missing her at some point during it. Forty or fifty years apart might do it.

But she deserved to be able to move on. He didn't have the right to stand in her way.

He was going stir-crazy in this office. Reid cursed and threw his pen down on the desk blotter so hard it bounced off and landed on the carpet. He had to get out for a while. There were a dozen more calls to be made. Several documents to be signed and countless emails to answer. But he couldn't concentrate. Before the start of this week he might have boasted about his superior focus skills. It didn't help that he kept checking his phone to see if Celeste had sent him the text yet. As of three minutes ago, she had not. The short time frame didn't stop him from checking yet again. Nothing.

Not from her, anyway. By cruel contrast, his phone was buzzing with texts and voice mails left by his father.

He stood up and stormed out of his office. The desk attendant in the concierge area smiled at him when he approached. "Reid. I was just about to come knock. Someone left a file for you."

She handed him an envelope. He removed the papers within. Celeste's report. But she was supposed to have sent it electronically.

"How long ago was this dropped off?"

"Just a couple of minutes. The young lady used the business office to print it then dropped it off here. She said you were expecting it."

She couldn't have gotten far. Reid knew he shouldn't do it, but he found himself following the path she would take if she were to head back to her room from the concierge lobby. The least he could do was thank her.

The mocking voice reemerged. *As if that's the reason you're trying to catch her.*

He saw her moments later on the path by the kiddie pool. She stopped to retrieve and toss back an inflatable ball to a toddler when it rolled by her feet. The action stalled her long enough for him to catch up.

"Celeste." She froze.

"Reid?"

"Hey." He lifted the envelope in his hand. "Thanks for bringing this by."

"The text I attached it to kept bouncing back. The file must have been too big."

That explained the printout. He could release any notion that she might have come by the office hoping to run into him. He should have discounted that possibility in the first place. She had left it for him at the counter after all.

"Oh. Thanks for taking the time to print it out, then." How many times could he thank her in one conversation? He had no reason to be this tongue-tied around her. He had to get a grip already.

"You're welcome."

The toddler threw the ball back at her. Celeste flashed the child a bright smile and tossed the toy back once more.

"I'm looking forward to reading it," he told her when she'd turned back to him.

"I hope it helps."

"There's still the matter of your compensation. I can have papers drawn up—"

She held a hand up before he could continue. "That won't be necessary. I won't accept any type of payment from you."

A boulder settled in his chest. Part of him was convinced she'd take him up on the free annual vacations. That he would at least be able to see her again once every year. Though he'd feel gutted every time she left. "I don't understand. I don't feel right having you do all this work for nothing."

The ball landed between their feet again. They both turned to find the same toddler boy giggling.

Come on, pal, Reid thought, groaning inside. This was hard enough without a toothless lothario intent on a game of catch with his woman.

His woman?

He cleared his throat. "I'd like to talk about this."

She gave a slight lift of her shoulder. "If you wish. Sure, we can talk. But I won't change my mind."

Reid quickly took her by the elbow and led her to the poolside cabana bar before the beach ball reappeared. Celeste allowed him to guide her onto one of the stools. He motioned for the bartender and ordered two rum punches. He never drank during the day when he was working. But this was an extenuating circumstance if ever he'd encountered one.

He'd missed her. It had only been a few hours since he'd left her this morning. But he couldn't deny that he'd spent those hours wishing she was still by his side. He missed her smile, her wit. The way she smelled.

"Tell me why," he said once their icy drinks had arrived.

Celeste took a swig from her paper straw and his gaze immediately fell to her lips.

"I thought we had an agreement," he added.

"I've changed my mind. Consider it professional courtesy on my part. As your resort guest."

So that's all she was going to classify herself as. He had no business being disappointed. He wanted this distance, didn't he? It's why he had fled her room after the night they'd spent together.

For such a hot, pleasant day, they were the only two people seated at the bar. The bartender was busy at work several feet away with his back to them organizing bottles and tidying.

If they were a real couple, Reid might take the opportunity to kiss her.

His cell phone started to vibrate in his shirt pocket before he took that thought any further. He quickly removed the device and set it to do not disturb, ignoring the risk of missing an important business call. And if it was his father calling yet again...well, he'd had enough of his father's interruptions for a lifetime.

"I don't mind," Celeste said, pointing to his phone on the bar. "You can answer that, if you want."

"I don't want."

She lifted an eyebrow in question. "Oh?"

Reid blew out a deep breath. "I'm in the middle of something rather unpleasant. It involves my father. He wants to talk about it. Only there's nothing left to talk about."

"Ah." Celeste took another sip of her drink. "If it makes you feel better, I wish I hadn't received a call from my own parent this morning."

He laughed. "Yeah?"

"Oh, yeah. It was a doozy."

"Maybe we'll have to compare notes on our parents someday."

She ducked her head, suddenly serious. "I'd rather not."

"Tell me something," she asked, not meeting his eyes.

"Yes?"

"You said before that you and Jack didn't talk at all about me after we broke up."

Where was this all leading? Reid had no idea. He only knew that the reminder that she'd once been engaged to another man had his gut tightening. He really had no desire to talk about her ex-fiancé. "That's right."

"What about before the breakup? You two must have talked about the woman he was about to marry."

He shrugged, still confused about the direction this conversation had taken. He'd sat her down to try to convince her to accept payment for her hard work.

"What did he tell you about me, Reid? Did he say I was just after his money?"

He hadn't seen that question coming at all, wasn't sure how to answer. If he thought hard about it, Reid would have to admit that Jack had in fact insinuated that very thing. "Celeste, what's this all about?"

She took another sip from her straw, looked away toward the crystal-blue water of the pool. "See, he would have been right to say so if he did. It's the real reason he left me."

CHAPTER FIFTEEN

CELESTE COULDN'T REALLY say if her intention had been to shock Reid. But it sure looked like she'd done just that.

She hadn't had anything to eat all day, just that pot of coffee this morning. And the rum punch was so much stronger than any drink she was used to. Combined with the confusion that seeing Reid always seemed to bring forth within her, the alcohol had gone straight to her head and loosened her lips.

Reid suddenly stood. Dropping several bills onto the bar, he picked up his cell phone and the report. Then he gently nudged her up out of her stool.

"Let's go."

Celeste followed without question. The cat was out of the bag now. Might as well get everything out in the open.

He led her to a rental cabana that must not have been reserved for the day and pulled down the privacy flaps. A shiver of apprehension ran down Celeste's spine when he turned and fixed his gaze on her.

"Care to explain?" he demanded.

She dropped down onto the padded lounger and studied her toes. "I didn't grow up with any money, Reid. Unlike the way you and Jack grew up."

"Don't make assumptions, Celeste."

"What does that mean?"

But he wasn't going to allow the switch in topic. "Never mind. We're talking about you."

She let out a deep breath. "Why do you think Jack decided he couldn't go through with the wedding?"

"He got cold feet. It happens."

She laughed without any real mirth behind it. "He got cold feet because my mother and sister made no secret of the fact that they were very excited about how rich he was. They acted downright giddy."

Nausea roiled through her stomach at the memories. There'd been times when Momma had come right out and asked Jack about his net worth and how much he was willing to part with to help his future in-laws.

The humiliation had been unbearable.

She sucked in a deep breath. "Jack insisted we needed to get away from my mother and sister, starting with the wedding. Hence the desire to elope—so they wouldn't be there. He also suggested we consider living on the West Coast afterward. To stay far away from them."

"You said no."

"In no uncertain terms. I'm all the family Tara and my mother have. There is no one else. I couldn't just turn my back on them."

Reid remained silent, simply waited for her to continue.

"So Jack can't really be faulted for walking away, can he?" she asked. "I can't really blame him."

Reid crossed his arms in front of his chest as he analyzed her. "Is that what you really think?"

She could only nod silently, still staring at her toes.

"What about the fact that he waited until the last minute to do it? Or how cowardly it was to leave you waiting there with a church full of guests? Can you blame him for any of those things?"

"I'm not saying he's a saint. I'm not defending him. And I'm not defending my mother and sister. I'm just saying I understand why he did it."

"No, you're just finding ways to blame yourself. For the cowardly way he treated you. For the way your family members treated you. None of which had anything to do with *you*."

He emphasized the last word with heavy inflection.

Suddenly, anger and frustration flooded her chest. She hadn't confided in him to be scrutinized or lectured to or somehow analyzed.

"Spare me the empty platitudes, Reid. I'm not telling you any of this to garner some sort of sympathy or for your pity."

"Then why did you tell me?"

"So that you know why I can't keep coming back here year after year. Seeing you again. That part of the deal is absolutely off the table."

She sucked in a labored breath. "And there's absolutely no way I'll take any money from you. I just wanted you to understand why."

She brushed past him and rushed through the canvas flap before he could see how close to breaking down she really was.

He didn't try to follow her.

Celeste hadn't stopped shaking by the time she reached her room and slammed the door shut. Her gaze immediately fell to the bed, bringing forth haunting and erotic images of all that she and Reid had shared the night before. How foolish she had been to fall in love with a man who was so terribly wrong for her. Her heart felt heavy and bruised in her chest. Like someone had struck a physical blow. She didn't know if the ache would ever heal. Her breakup with Jack had been a hard hit to her ego. The loss she felt now felt like an open wound, one she might never recover from.

But now wasn't the time to dwell on any of that. She had a call to make. With shaky fingers, she reached for her phone and clicked on her mother's contact icon.

Wendy picked up after several rings. "Did you pay the bill?"

Not even a hello. Why was she even surprised?

"Momma. Listen to me. There's something very important I need to explain to you."

Celeste didn't give her mother a chance to protest. She just calmly and distinctly went over the decisions she'd recently made. Then she clearly explained the steps she planned to take in implementing them all.

Her determination must have rung through clearly in Celeste's voice because her mother didn't argue. In fact, Celeste thought she might even have heard a tinge of relief in Wendy's voice.

The perfect setting to fall in love...speaking from personal experience...

Reid reread the same passages from the file Celeste had turned in yet once more. He'd lost count how many times he'd already read them. As a marketing plan, she'd handed him pure gold. Her suggestions were sound, and many of her ideas could justifiably be described as brilliant. But those were the only lines he cared about.

She'd made it personal. And she was telling him she'd fallen in love with him. He was glad he'd made it back to his living quarters before taking the time to read her report. Something had told him he should be alone while looking at the file, someplace he wouldn't risk being interrupted. Finally putting the papers down, he walked over to the wet bar across the sitting area and poured himself a generous amount of aged dark rum.

She loved him. It said so in black and white. Written by her hand.

Lord knew he didn't deserve it. That he fell far short of the type of man someone like Celeste was worthy of. So now the only question was what was he going to do about it?

He downed the rum all at once, felt the satisfying burn of the spirit travel down his throat. It did nothing to ease his inner turmoil.

He'd called her ex a coward earlier today in the beachside cabana when he'd pulled her in there after her so-called "admission." He had to examine whether he was the one being cowardly now. Was he going to let her walk off this island in a few short days and out of his life for good? Or was he going to be as brave as she was? The woman had fearlessly laid it all on the line by putting her feelings into words that the whole world was meant to see.

He wasn't worthy of such a selfless act done on his behalf. But he'd been bestowed with it nonetheless. He couldn't walk away. He would find her, and they would determine once and for all how to move forward. Together.

He had so much upheaval in his life right now, had no guarantee what the future held if this deal didn't work. His father was hell-bent on bleeding the company dry. He could only hope the board saw that fact and sided with him.

Because damned if he hadn't just realized that he'd fallen in love with her, too. He needed to tell her so. It was only right. He needed to follow her example and be as courageous as she was. He also needed to take her into his arms and make sure she understood that he was never going to let her go.

But first, a shower. It had been a long, grueling day that had left tension knotting in his shoulders and back.

Reid couldn't help the smile that tugged at his mouth as he walked to the bathroom and turned the water on. In a few short hours, if all went well and he could persuade Celeste to listen, he'd be holding her and kissing her again. That had to make him the luckiest man in the universe.

He realized all too soon that the universe had other plans.

Reid's phone lit up like a Christmas tree when he left the shower fifteen minutes later. With a chest full of trepidation, he returned the call to the number that had been trying to reach him for the entire time he'd been bathing.

One of his lawyers.

This was not a good sign.

The attorney answered on the first ring. "Bad news, Reid. We're going to need to do some damage control or you run the real risk of reverting all control back to Dale."

"I take it my father has managed to push through a vote?"

"You'd be right. You need to fly down to Boston first thing."

Reid disconnected the call and cursed the fates he'd been so sure were smiling on him just minutes before.

He tapped out Celeste's number on his screen but she didn't answer. His intended message wasn't the kind a man left on voice mail. He would have to try to get a hold of her later.

Right now, he had a flight to book and packing to do.

* * *

Celeste tried to focus on the same book she'd been trying to read ever since she'd arrived on the island. She'd barely gotten through the first couple of chapters. As gripping as the plot was, she couldn't seem to find herself immersed in the story.

She was much too distracted wondering whether Reid had read the file yet. There seemed to be no good conclusion. If he hadn't looked at it yet, what exactly was he waiting for? Why was he putting it off?

And if he had read it but wasn't reaching out to her… That scenario was the more heartbreaking possibility.

Well, she'd done all she could. She'd laid herself bare. Both with what she'd written and everything she'd told him in the cabana earlier. There was nothing more of her to expose to the man. Regardless of his ultimate reactions, she vowed to never regret her decision to do so.

She needed something to take her mind off him. The book wasn't cutting it. Celeste reached for her phone and dialed her sister's number. The gurgling, happy sounds of her baby niece would be like Uma's balm to her injured soul.

"Hey, Tara," she spoke into the phone when her sister answered. "How are you?"

"All right, putting up Nat's first Christmas

tree. She's very confused about why there's a tree in the house. And why I'm hanging shiny things off its branches."

Celeste had to laugh at that. Maybe her little niece would be enough of a reason from now on to stay in New York for the holidays in the future. "I really miss the little tyke."

"She misses you, too."

"Can you put her on the phone? I just wanna hear her make noises for a bit. Maybe get her to say CeeCee again."

Her sister laughed. "I think you imagined that. She is not trying to say your name already. She's only nine months old."

"I heard it loud and clear that day!" she exclaimed with a laugh.

"In any case, I'm afraid she's down for a nap right now."

"Oh. That's too bad." Celeste wasn't prepared for the depth of the disappointment she felt at the news. She really had missed the little girl, hadn't realized exactly how much until now.

Tara paused a beat before continuing. "You sound sad, sis. What is it?"

A sensation of warmth blossomed in her chest. She and Tara had their differences…what siblings didn't? But they somehow always knew how to read each other and tried to cheer each other up when it was called for.

"Nothing. And everything," she admitted.

"Does 'everything' include Ma?"

"So, you heard huh?"

"Yeah, she called here right after you told her. She knows it's the right thing to do. For what it's worth, I think you did the right thing, too."

Celeste sat upright on the bed. "You do?"

"Yeah. She's gotten bad. Doesn't pay attention to how much she's spending or what she's spending it on. She needs someone else to take charge of her finances. It might curb her drinking, too. Which also seems way out of hand lately."

"I set up an annuity for her," Celeste explained. "She'll get a certain amount every month as spending money. But I'll be the one in charge of her expenditures. And she has to agree to register for an addiction counseling service."

"I think that's wise." Tara hesitated before continuing. "Along those same lines, I've also been meaning to thank you. For setting up that trust for the baby. You know I appreciate it, right? And she will, too."

"I know, Tara."

This conversation was getting way too heavy. Celeste decided to change the subject. Though the next topic wasn't such a light one either.

"How's the job search going?" she asked, knowing there couldn't be much of one.

Tara audibly sobbed into the phone. "Tara? Are you crying?" Not Tara, too! What was it with her family and all the waterworks today?

She heard a sniffle. "Maybe."

"What's wrong?"

"I just can't take it, sis. Those office buildings, sitting in those cubicles. It's not me. I feel stifled and caged. But office work is the only thing I'm qualified for."

Oh, dear. Celeste had no idea her sister felt that way. How had she never thought to ask? What kind of big sister did that make her?

None of which had anything to do with you.

Reid's words echoed in her head. He'd been right. This was about Tara, not about herself. She needed to find a way to separate herself from the needs of her family.

"What do you want to be qualified for?"

Another sniffle. "I don't know. But remember all those pictures I used to take before that camera Uncle Zed got us finally broke?"

The question invoked a vague memory in her mind. But apparently, the camera had meant a great deal to her sister. "Yes."

"I really enjoyed taking those pictures."

"You did?"

"Yeah, I did. And I was good at it, too. But

you know how Ma is. She told me we didn't have the money to replace the camera. And that it was a stupid waste of time anyway."

That certainly sounded like their mother. Celeste had been so focused on her own treatment at her mother's hands, she'd completely missed the negativity that Tara had grown up with.

The answer came to her without question. "Then it's about time we replaced that camera, Tara." She told her sister. "And maybe we can find you a class that can show you how to take even better photos."

Her sister's gratitude came through loud and clear in her cheer of delight. "That's always been a dream of mine," Tara squealed into the phone. Again, Celeste had to wonder why she was first hearing this now.

"Careful," Celeste warned. "You'll wake up the baby."

Tara laughed. "I should probably go check on her. But just one more thing, sis."

"What's that?"

"I don't know why you sound so sad, you're on vacation in paradise, after all. But you deserve to have your dreams happen, too."

CHAPTER SIXTEEN

YOU DESERVE TO have your dreams happen, too.

Tara's voice still echoed in her mind the following morning. Celeste showered quickly then quickly got dressed and threw on her sandals. She fled out the door before she could change her mind. Step one in pursuing a dream was to have the courage to ask for what you wanted.

She wanted Reid.

Unlike the previous days since her arrival, this morning's sky was cloudy and gray. The air was thick with muggy moisture. She would guess a rainstorm was headed their way soon. Hopefully, the weather wasn't any kind of ominous sign regarding what she was about to do. When she reached the concierge level, she made a beeline straight to Reid's door. She had to do this before she lost her nerve.

Her knock went unanswered. She tried again with the same result. A pleasant male voice sounded behind her. "Can I help you with something, Celeste?"

She turned to face Reid's smiling, handsome business partner, Alex.

"I, um, was looking for Reid."

"Maybe I can help you."

She quickly shook her head. "I don't think so. I did some work for him, I just wanted to get his feedback on it." She had to tell the lie. She couldn't exactly divulge to Alex the real reason she was here. Kind eyes or not.

"Ah, right."

She shifted awkwardly. "Do you happen to know when he'll be in today?" she asked, knowing she sounded anxious and impatient but unable to help it.

"I'm afraid he won't be in at all today. I actually don't know when he'll be back. He flew out to Boston earlier this morning."

Celeste would have sunk into the floor if she didn't have an audience. Reid had left. Without so much as a goodbye. He hadn't even tried to find her first.

Alex continued to speak. She barely heard him over the pounding in her ears. "But I know he's read your file," he told her. "I'm sure he'll email you his comments in due time."

Celeste felt as if the wind had been knocked out of her lungs. Reid was going to email his comments. She'd laid her heart out on those pages. And he didn't think enough of that to so much as try to talk to her about it. He'd run off. Just like Jack had done on the day of their wedding.

Ridiculous as it sounded, Reid's betrayal felt like the bigger one by far. She'd recovered from Jack's desertion. She knew the same wasn't going to be possible this time.

She did her best to summon a smile for Reid's friend. "Thank you. I'll look for it in my inbox."

She could do so on her way to the airport. Looked like she would be cutting her trip short. She no longer had any desire to stay.

Or to ever come back again.

In his anxiousness and relief to be back in Jamaica, Reid exited the town car almost before the vehicle had come to a complete stop in the circular driveway of the Baja Majestic.

This had to be the quickest trip he'd ever taken to Boston and back. He usually booked at least one night at the Evanson Premier Boston Harbor hotel before taking a morning flight the next day. But he'd had no intention of sticking around the city this time. Once the confrontation with his father was over, he was more than ready to fly back to the Caribbean. Back to the resort he'd called home for weeks now. Back to Celeste. They had quite a bit to work out between them.

Though confrontation wasn't exactly the correct term for the meeting he'd had with Dale. Reid had arrived at Evanson Properties headquarters just in time to head off a vote of the board of directors. The clear relief on the expressions of the twelve executives told him the vote could have gone either way.

After that, he'd made sure to finally have the one-to-one with his father that he'd been avoiding for so long. It had taken Celeste to help him discover his avoidance had been more personal than business. He had yet to thank her for that.

In the end, Dale had seen reason and agreed to a limited role as a company president. Another weight lifted off Reid's shoulders, though he and his father had a long way to go before their personal relationship could begin to mend.

All in due time.

Nodding to the doorman, he passed through the sliding doors into the Baja Majestic lobby, gratified that several guests were milling about, ready to check in. So far, the holiday season could officially be called a success. Celeste's marketing plan would only help once it was implemented. Yet another thank-you she was due.

He stopped at the counter and removed his sunglasses. "Sanya, please deliver a cart with our finest champagne and a variety of desserts to Room B717."

The woman behind the counter smiled and started clicking at the computer keyboard in front of her. "Right away, sir." Her smile suddenly flattened with confusion. "Is that the correct room, Mr. Evanson?"

"Yes. Is there a problem?"

She returned her gaze to the monitor screen. "Our system says the room is empty, housekeeping is in there now. The guest has already checked out."

Reid felt all the excitement he'd experienced only moments before extinguish like a blown-out flame, replaced with a pounding sense of disappointment and hurt.

She was gone.

If she kept busy enough, and took on enough projects, she could almost push Reid Evanson out of her mind for several minutes at a time. The only problem was, the days between Christmas and New Year's didn't exactly bring in a lot of business activity. Still, Celeste made it a point to go into her Upper East Side office in every morning to find ways to keep herself busy. Never mind that she was one of only a few people there. Most of the other employees were out preparing to celebrate New Year's Eve.

So far, she'd gone over all her deliverables for the new year, and then she'd gone over them again. She'd studied past successful campaigns to analyze what had worked and why.

She'd even cleared out her inbox and organized her paper files via a new method. Today she figured she might tackle cleaning out the break room.

Despite the relatively empty floor, a flurry of noise drew her attention from outside her door. What was that all about?

The commotion drew closer to her door. "Ho-ho-ho!"

She stood from her desk and opened her door. Someone dressed as Santa appeared to be approaching her office. Celeste rubbed at her temples. How had this guy gotten past Security? There were no children's daycares or anything of the sort on this floor. Not to mention Christmas was already over, thankfully.

"I think you're lost, Santa," she addressed St. Nick, her phone in her hand ready to call Security if need be.

His response was to reach for his jaw and pull down the pretend beard and mustache—to reveal the face she'd been dreaming of since she'd left Jamaica all those days ago.

"Reid?"

"Hi, sweetheart."

Celeste had to brace herself against the wall at her back. She couldn't be seeing or hearing any of this. She must be having some kind of *A Christmas Carol* hallucination or dream. Tiny Tim would pop out any minute now.

She blinked and rubbed her eyes. But Reid still stood there. As real as the hammering of her heart.

"What are you doing here?" she stammered out.

"I had an emergency business trip to make right before the holiday. As soon as I successfully wrapped it up, I realized I didn't get a chance to wish my lady a Merry Christmas."

His lady?

"You flew out here just to wish me a Merry Christmas?"

They'd drawn the attention of the few other people who'd come into work. Her colleagues were staring at them in astonishment. Two of the women looked like they were dabbing at their eyes.

"I did," Reid answered her, walking closer until he stood mere inches away. How did the man manage to look sexy in a bulky Santa suit, for heaven's sake? It took all her will not to throw her arms around him and nuzzle her face into his neck. She'd missed him so much, still couldn't believe this wasn't some fantasy or dream she'd be waking up from any minute now.

"Oh, I also wanted to give your Christmas present. Didn't get a chance to do that, either."

He reached inside the pocket of his red fleece pants. Then shocked her to her core by pulling out a velvet box and dropping to one knee.

Flipping the top over, he revealed a sparkling diamond ring surrounded by dazzling ruby red stones. He'd been thinking of the black-and-red dress she'd worn the night of the dinner cruise. There was no doubt in her mind.

Celeste had to remind herself to breathe.

"Celeste Frajedi. You're unlike anyone else I've ever known."

Her voice shook as she tried to answer. "I am?"

"Without a doubt. I would call you the most generous person I've ever met. And I'd like to call you my wife." He took her shaking hand in his. "Will you marry me?"

She couldn't stand any more. Literally. Celeste felt her knees give out and Reid caught her as she dropped to the floor in front of him.

"Yes!" She'd barely gotten the word out when applause and cheers erupted all around them.

"I can't believe this is happening," she said over all the noise. "I can't believe that you're really here."

"I am, sweetheart. And I want to promise you that I'll do everything I can to make sure each

Christmas we celebrate together is more festive than the last."

That settled it. Her tears would not be contained any longer. The love she felt for this man overflowed through every part of her being. "Oh, Reid."

"It's like a wise newlywed once said…" He laughed, taking her in his arms and hugging her tight. "When you know you're with the right person, you just know."

Celeste knew. Just as she knew that the holidays would hold magic and happiness for her once again.

* * * * *

*If you enjoyed this story,
check out these other great reads
from Nina Singh*

Swept Away by the Venetian Millionaire
Captivated by the Millionaire
Christmas with Her Secret Prince
Tempted by Her Island Millionaire

All available now!